Bottom of the Heap

Reeti Gadekar was born and brought up in New Delhi. She studied German literature and now lives in Berlin, Germany. *Bottom of the Heap* is her second novel. Her first novel, *Families at Home,* was short-listed for the Man Asian Literary Prize in 2007.

Bottom of the Heap

Reeti Gadekar

HarperCollins *Publishers* India

First published in India by
HarperCollins *Publishers* in 2010

Building 10, Tower A, 4th Floor, DLF Cyber City, Phase II,

Gurugram Haryana – 122002, India

www.harpercollins.co.in

2 4 6 8 10 9 7 5 3

P-ISBN: 978-81-7223-977-0
E-ISBN: 978-93-5029-312-6

Typeset in 11/15 Calisto MT
InoSoft Systems

Printed and bound at
MicroPrints India, New Delhi

Happy Birthday, SNji
05.08.2010

15 September 1999

Road Construction Hit by Pilferage

New Delhi: The Centre has been requested to help local authorities in a case of petty pilferage and theft in the Miraat/Pankot area. The Singh family, which has been holding land and other property for generations in this area, was planning the construction of a road which would hugely benefit this otherwise backward region. It is hoped that the Centre will facilitate investigation so that locals and outsiders alike can gain from the new road.

No Rollback i[illegible] Diesel

German Raped by Cop in India's Rape Capital

New Delhi: In yet another shocking incident of violence, a German woman was allegedly molested in the Basantpur police station by Constable Sajjan Kumar late last evening. Delhi Police has promised a speedy inquiry. Violence against women has long been a problem in Delhi, the rape capital of India. Since last year, the rape statistics have shown an upward swing in Delhi, while in neighbouring states the statistics

cont. pg. 27.

10 October 1999

An Arse Full of Rape

New Delhi: In the village of Arse, police officers have shown their true colours: they are attackers and violators of women, not their protectors.

Three women were in police custody in a petty-crime case. They were brutally attacked and left for dead. Two bodies were found mutilated and violated whereas one is believed to have survived the heinous attack.

The whereabouts of the women (or their bodies) is currently under investigation. Who will now investigate this case? The perpetrators, aka the police, themselves?

The Centre is allegedly considering taking the case into its own hands. But is it really in a position to do anything? Or is the gesture just a case of one-upmanship and name calling between a pot and a kettle? Delhi is the unenviable rape capital of the country and the Centre has time and again proven to be helpless against the rising tide of violence in the city.

A few weeks ago, Delhi had made headlines with the Theresa Schmidt case. Constable Sajjan Kumar, who was under investigation for that particularly barbaric crime is said to be safe since he is allegedly under the aegis of Additional Commissioner Nikhil Juneja. Is it then a coincidence that Nikhil Juneja was in Arse some days back? And where was his faithful assistant, Sajjan Kumar?

1 October 1999

'Road scam?'

'Yes, sir.'

'What do you mean by road scam?'

'Sir, I don't know, sir.'

Sinha looked highly despondent as he well might. Road scam? Was Gupta out of his mind? He, Nikhil Juneja, the sweetheart of the masses, the best-loved detective of them all, the *it* policeman would now go off to the back of beyond to check out a road scam? What was a road scam? How could you scam a road?

'OK, get out. And make some coffee, I'll call you.'

It wasn't fair. The world was unfair. Why? Why must the world be unfair? The file was almost impossible to understand. Some rubbish about tar and roadrollers and a town ... or was it a village? Basically some bum joint out in the boondocks. Juneja calmed down slightly. It was the first of a decidedly cool October. He was still basking in the success of his last case and a road scam was perhaps better than running around morgues and maybe it was in Goa and he'd get to celebrate New Year's on the beach for free.

Juneja shrugged. Could be fun. Only thing, in Goa, a sex scam would have been better. He would even have been willing to settle for a dope scam. Some teenage chick, foreign, hot, who slowly developed the hots for him. It would have been fun. The Indian press didn't think much of foreign chicks who came to India in skimpy clothes anyway. The idea was that tiny clothes were begging to be ripped off, a thought Juneja pretty much concurred with. He sighed. Alas! Such clothes didn't seem to be coming his way in a hurry.

He rang the bell for Sinha, who waddled back in a little faster than usual. Sign of winter approaching. In the summer, when the police station was a furnace, Sinha could not be trusted to move fast. However, come winter, he moved at 3 km/h, a vast improvement on his summer speed.

'Sir? Coffee is just ready.'

'Good. Get me two packets of Marlboros. When does Gupta Sir want to see me?'

'Sir, Gupta Sir said that you should look through the file to be prepared for the meeting today in the afternoon at two o'clock, sir.'

'Two? It's bloody twelve forty-five now, you ass!'

'Sir, I told you—'

'No, you didn't, you bloody—'

'Sir, I tried, sir, but sir, you get outed me. But I know, sir, Gupta Sir should not have given you a file so thick, sir, but sir, he said sir, that Juneja Sir should get fixed.'

Juneja leant back. Now that was a development. Could Sinha be trusted? 'Get fixed' or 'fix it'?

'Go away and get the stuff, alright?

'The fags, sir?'

'The fags? What do you mean fags?'

'Sir, Joseph's daughter told me, Elizabeth, that in proper English, cigarettes are called fags. Why are they called fags, sir?'

'Because, Sinha, you are a bloody faggot.'

'Yes, sir.'

Could it be true? Gupta wanted him fixed? Was his senior, already joint commissoner, Gupta trying deviously to put the skids on his career? The only thing standing between him and his promotion was a woman … Sanjana was almost calling herself his girlfriend on the telephone. Well, she had called him *her* guy. Once. She had told him quite clearly that she had no intention of marrying a policeman. Probably because it was so much cooler being Mrs Juneja Fabrics. So, it was either Juneja Fabrics and Sanjana or no Juneja Fabrics and no Sanjana. Besides, who was he kidding? Sanjana and the massive boobs? *Breasts, Nikhil, breasts.* Sanjana had been enraged that he should call her boobs, boobs, or rather her breasts, boobs. Breasts always reminded him of ducks. And that wasn't sexy. She was coming down to Delhi from the US for Christmas. For good, after four years.

He thought they could go down to Goa to usher in the New Year. The new era in his life, where for the first time on New Year's Eve he wouldn't be sitting in front of the television or be on the verge of passing out at some useless party without women. This time round, he might pop a question. *The* question.

Were the good times coming to an end before they'd even begun?

'Sir, cold fags with hot coffee, sir.'

Juneja drew a deep breath. It could hardly get worse than this.

'Thank you, Sinha. Also, get out.'

Joint Commissioner Gupta's new office was a tad larger than his old one. Rumour had it that Gupta had even put in an application for an air-conditioner. *Bastard*. But the true advantage lay in the fact that he no longer faced the garbage dump. His old office had been converted into the new 'temporary detention room'. It was a kind of pre-softening process. Close the windows and let the sods die in gasps in their own stench. Sajjan Kumar, Juneja's most prized assistant, aka the Prince of Brutality, had suggested it.

His current office was in the annexe. The old building had been bursting at the seams; hence, a new one had been suggested. But it was hard to believe that this crappy annexe would take any of the pressure off. Construction had started during the monsoon months. God alone knows why. The contractor who had been paid a pretty packet in cash probably did, but wasn't telling. He was allegedly the nephew of joint commissioner, traffic. *You scam my back, I scam yours.*

It was now clear that the building was woefully inadequate. There was only one toilet, no storage space and some of the rooms had no windows at all, leading to a slow but steady death by baking. The staff was coping with the massive amount of paperwork or scam work in the usual way: piling it in the corridor. If nothing else, it could always be used to mop up the copious amounts of water that was destined to come through, either next year during the monsoon or this winter, should the rain god be extra merciful. By that time, bloody Gupta would probably have himself another office, built by the nephew of the joint commissioner, training.

As he approached the office, he discovered Sajjan Kumar sitting in a corner, smoking.

'What are you doing here?'

'Sir, Gupta Sir called me.'

Juneja nodded and made his way to the office. This was a good sign. Obviously, Sajjan Kumar had been called to assist him. Sajjan Kumar was barely literate and with his kind of fists, didn't need to be. He could fix any road, scammed or skinned.

'Come in, Nikhil! My boy, come in! Arre, how have you been?' Ever since his last success, Gupta had started using his first name. At least when they were alone. Very embarrassing.

'Very well, thank you, sir.'

'Recovered from your last case, hmm? Come in, come in!'

How much more could he come in? The room looked larger than it was, given that it contained only a small round table and four unoccupied chairs. Was this to be a conference room?

'Have you had a chance to look at the file?'

Juneja had no qualms about this one at all. 'Not really, sir. Sinha got mixed up and handed it over to me at one thirty. I tried to have a look, but unfortunately—'

'Not to worry, Nikhil, not to worry. Sit down. Will you have tea or coffee? This meeting could go on.'

Juneja was up to the challenge. Never sit till your senior has; merely hover near the chair, so he stops prattling about sitting down. Sitting down would be a breach of etiquette. But hovering had to be done discreetly. You had to time sitting down; such that your ass touched the cushion a second after Senior Ass hit the chair. And the idea was to make sure that Senior Ass realized that you sat only *after* he sat down.

'Whatever is convenient, sir. I am sure the coffee and the tea here will be much better. After all it is the office of the joint commissioner!'

A little obvious ass licking never hurt.

'Arre, Nikhil, you will be joint commissioner yourself very soon! What are you worried about? Now stop hoovering and sit down, hmm?'

Hoovering? No, nothing could be worse.

'Well, Nikhil, this is a very good case. Very good. I have got word from the top that you should get it,' announced Gupta once they had settled down with the file.

Did that mean his father? Juneja tried to look solemn, but there was a twinkle in Gupta's eye that belied the goodness of the case. Was the bastard really trying to get rid of him?

'Nikhil, this case is good in two ways. Firstly ...'

Gupta sauntered off, mid-sentence, to the window in an effort to remember the importance of the case.

'Firstly, my boy, this case is good. You know, there are all these small murders and things happening but these are, in the long term, not good. But this case is *good*. It should get cleared up quite fast and show the department in a good light.'

'Right.'

'And secondly, this case is good for you. For you personally. You will make new, important contacts, meet people who can perhaps help you in your career.'

Gupta paused again. This time to contemplate the surface of the table, which he carefully scrutinized for long, painful moments. Juneja felt his nerves jangle.

'Yes, Nikhil, it is good for you. I have, yes, I have also spoken to your father.'

My father? Bastard. Bastards. You and him.

'He says he wants you to think about leaving the police and joining the business.'

Juneja felt his stomach constrict painfully.

'Joining the business?'

He didn't realize he'd spoken out aloud.

Gupta had stopped surveying the room in general and was now looking straight at him. There was a great deal of empathy in his tone.

'Nikhil, it wouldn't be a bad thing if you did ... but that is really your decision. I have nothing to do with it. But with this road scam, you would have a chance of ending your career with the police on a high note. You father's health has been quite problematic in the recent past and I know he wants you to come back to the family business before he, he ... Well, during his lifetime,' ended Gupta lamely.

'Why should I end my career?'

'Fine, don't. Stay with the police till the end. But you still need a good case to make it up the ladder. Arre, Nikhil, it's a great case. You haven't had a chance to study the file; that is why you think there will be a problem. Have a look at it and you will be more at ease. I'd suggest you take a new officer as your assistant to crack this case!'

Juneja closed his eyes. Maybe when he opened them, Gupta would have disappeared. Failing which, he could close his eyes again and imagine the *case* of Gupta's brain being *cracked*.

A knock on the door preceded the pots of tea. Juneja tried not to shudder at the sight of radioactive orange liquid in chipped cups straight out of the gutter. Stay with these losers? He could barely manage to drink tea with them.

Juneja walked back to his office in a trance. Sinha moved at a surprising speed to usher him into his office but Juneja stopped him.

'No, I, umm, I need the roster. Send it in, no, give it to me. I'm standing here.'

Sinha looked at him, nonplussed.

'Yes,' repeated Juneja, 'I am standing here, bring it here. I'll wait.'

Sinha waddled away at a slick pace. He had been working with Juneja Sir for a long time. In this time, he had learnt many things about Juneja and about the police force in general. You never keep your superior waiting. Juneja would wait, as he said, but then he would wait and later kick your ass. There was no fairness in the world.

On this occasion it was easy to find the roster. It was Friday and the roster was in the reception area, so that changes could be made at the end of the day for the week to come. In fact, Juneja could have picked it up on his way in. Not that he, Sinha, would ever dream of telling him this.

All told, he was feeling quite depressed. His colleague Sajjan Kumar had not come back with Juneja. A sure sign that he had not been allotted this case. Another pal of his, K. Joseph, was going home to Kerala for Christmas. It was a big thing for Christians, like their own Diwali. Well, since there weren't many Christians in the police station, Gupta Sir had given his kind permission vide letter dated 11 September 1999. Joseph was having a tough time persuading his wife, though. She claimed that Christmas in Delhi was better than in Kerala.

'Sir, roster, sir,' cooed Sinha to Juneja.

But Juneja was in a funny mood. He had remained standing at the door to his office and now he took the roster in an absent-minded sort of way.

'No, Sinha, no, I, umm, I need the roster, no, no a copy of the roster.'

'Yes, sir. You will wait again?' queried Sinha. 'Here in front of office?'

Juneja was surprised by the question. Was he in front of an office?

'No, Sinha, I am going to sit down here. I need to find another assistant for the new case. More paperwork involved. Sajjan Kumar won't do.' He sat down at Sinha's desk.

Appalled at the sight of Juneja slumping down on *his* desk, Sinha took off at the speed of light. What was wrong?

Although Sinha had not foreseen Sajjan Kumar's possible redundancy in a new case consisting hopefully of scams and paperwork, as far as he was concerned, it meant less running around and cleaning up dirty people after Sajjan Kumar had pissed on them.

Neither had he foreseen that Juneja could be unhappy about a case with more paperwork. After all, police work wasn't all dead bodies and rapes and who had done what. It could also be form-filling and sitting around and letting the others do the work ...

Sinha felt quite bad for Juneja who was obviously out of sorts. He made clean copies of the roster (Juneja could be rather particular) and hurried back.

He gave Juneja a tender, understanding smile as he extended the copies. 'Sir, roster copies, sir.'

Juneja, who had been sitting looking at nothing at all, was startled. He was about to bite off Sinha's silly grinning head but then he couldn't be bothered.

'Sinha, what case are you working on?'

Sinha was shocked. Him, work a case?

'Sir, no case, sir. But sir, I am doing arrangement for roster, sir ... and copies. And sir, also tea and coffee supplies and sir, Sajjan Kumar has gone to Gupta Sir for a new case, sir, and sir, I will have to supervise, sir.'

The last 'sir' had a desperate ring to it. Juneja smiled derisively. *Scum.*

'Get me fresh tea and two packets of cigarettes. And tell that bastard canteen owner, the tea is for me. It had better be fresh!'

'Yes, sir,' squeaked Sinha, happy to be on a mission he could cope with.

Juneja sauntered into his office feeling better now that he'd kicked some ass.

But, my boy, Nikhil, you too will pay for this scam. And boy will it cost. Juneja pulled himself back from going down that particularly slippery track.

No Sajjan Kumar. That bothered him. Sajjan Kumar was like an extension of himself ... in the worst possible way, but also in the most necessary way. He fulfilled basic needs. He provided brawn and crudity in a world of affected pretentiousness. With Sajjan, you could burp in peace. Discuss crude sex, knowing he'd always have had cruder. He beat up people for you, arranged for booze at unearthly hours ... the list was endless. He was the best grandmother ever!

No, Nikhil, out of the question. No way can you work with Sajjan Kumar. Although he was the answer to most problems; the one man fisting machine that opened all crevices, this case called for sensitivity, not a fist tank.

Boyo, you have to stop this! This isn't the time to be thinking of Sajjan Kumar's fists. This was the time to think about the case. Something he'd been trying without succeeding during the past twenty minutes, sitting at Sinha's smelly desk.

Scams were de rigueur in India. They'd had the big Harshad Mehta scam in the early '90s and it had ushered in the words *scam* and *scamster* into common lingo. Sure, in the past, people had cheated each other and taken each other for a ride, but post Mehta it was a scam.

If you had a chit fund and run away with everyone's money, it wasn't cheating or fraud, it was the Chit Fund Scam. Thus, one could have a fodder scam, a stamp-paper scam, a security scam or even a cobbler scam.

Juneja couldn't make sense of these scams, nor did he know anyone who did. But there were some things all scams had in common.

Fact One: All scams involve horrendous, simply horrendous sums of money. Not sixty-seven crores or any piddling sum like that. Your minimum scam starts at 150 crores plus. So, besides being unimaginably rich, you had to look for someone who was in a position to manipulate and administer money of this kind.

Fact Two: All scams involve the government. This is writ in stone. It may or may not make it easier to identify the said perp (as the Americans would say) or scamster (as the Indians did say) but it meant being very, very careful. Quite frankly he, Additional Commissioner Nikhil Juneja, hoping in the near future to finally become joint commissioner, found being careful a pain in the ass. On the other hand, catching a scamster, especially a political scamster, could also be a quick climb up the greasy pole. *You scam mine, I scam yours …*

Fact Three: All scams necessarily involve huge amounts of paperwork. Not on behalf of the idiots who'd done it and had been stupid enough to get caught. No, it was paperwork that he, Juneja, would have to wade through. It took a minimum of three years on an average to solve a scam, and all scamsters had the peculiar habit of camouflaging their ill-gotten wealth in a paper trail.

But the problem, the real problem was actually Fact Four: No one ever gets arrested in a scam. This too was writ in stone. After all, if your average idiot policeman/police force/investigating agency, etc. took three years investigating a scam, the investigation could hardly be kept a secret. This gave the alleged perp/scamster enough time—depending on whichever came first or cost the least—to wheedle his way out (read bribe) or develop a heart condition, or failing that, die, whereby he couldn't be jailed … which could be a good or a bad thing, depending on how the scam worked out. The political party the bugger belonged to could be in parliament next time round and then … *Yes, Nikhil, what bloody then? He'll screw your happiness. But what if his party isn't in power next time round? Then it's in power now, isn't it? So how do you arrest him? You don't. How do you get a leg-up? Hmm, you don't.*

Not a good answer.

A leg-up was essential.

He rang for Sinha, who came in looking woebegone.

His bloody problem.

'Is Sajjan Kumar back?'

'No, sir, not yet.'

'Send him in immediately.'

'Yes, sir.'

'And where are my two packets of Marlboro Lights and tea?'

'Sir, the chai-wallah is making fresh, sir, he is making, and I will bring immediately.'

Nikhil, you're forty-five and it's time you settled down. To a family and children and Juneja Fabrics which is branching out into exports and, for some strange reason best known to your father, car parts. Sanjana is thirty-seven and, let's face it, a little past her shelf life. How much longer can she procreate? As Uncle would put it, 'She's very mature. Too mature.' Sort of like lime pickle gone off. Soggy, smelly. What does that make you *at forty-five?*

He hadn't yet asked Sanjana about her pickled womb but he had made discreet inquiries via his best friend Rajiv, who had adopted kids some months ago. The children had come from an orphanage, twin girls. It hadn't stopped them from continuing to persevere with IVF, which according to Rajiv was hugely stressful and upsetting for his wife, Geetu.

Rajiv was ... never mind what he was, Nikhil. Why not go and see him? Why should you sit here and wait for Sajjan Kumar?

Nikhil rang for Sinha, who came bounding back in.

'Sir, Sajjan—'

'Yes, alright, he's not back. I need to go out on urgent business. You tell Gupta Sir, if he should ask, that my grandmother isn't feeling well. I'll try and come back later. OK?'

'OK, sir. Please give Mataji my best. And I will tell Sajjan Kumar to wait, sir?'

Finest supplication. Juneja felt his soul relax. *Why quit the police?*

The day was lukewarm; the sun couldn't quite decide whether it wanted earthlings in sweaters or shorts. Juneja got into his new car feeling distinctly discomfited. The Lancer was a gleaming red. Sanjana's choice. Juneja personally found it somewhat ill-suited to his age but what the hell; whatever made the little woman happy. The inside was however his choice. They'd waged Battle Royale over the beads on the seats. She insisted they were totally middle class. Juneja maintained he sweated less. She said that's what you have an AC for. Still, was his rejoinder. Also which member of the middle class could afford a Mitsubishi Lancer? Especially in crappy red? It made him feel like he was on fire.

Nikhil, you're meandering. What's wrong with you?

Nothing, nothing's wrong with me. I have a girlfriend and a new assignment and I'm going to see my best friend about adoption.

The last thought was so staggering, he stopped mid-movement.

No, no, I'm not. Why should I go and see Rajiv? I am not interested in children or adoption. I need to work on this case.

Juneja felt a huge surge of confidence. *Exactly*. He needed to find out how to crack the case as soon as possible; so that he could talk to his father about reconciliation and then maybe marriage, or at least a kind of settling down with Sanjana.

He marched back into the police station and discovered Sinha relaxing in a corner, gossiping on the telephone. He was so surprised to see Juneja back that the phone fell from his hand. Juneja made no effort to alleviate his discomfiture and gently pushed the phone out of Sinha's reach.

Juneja smiled. The sun shone.

'Who is this?'

'Sir, the peon from, you know, from there.'

'From Gupta's office?'

'Yes, sir.'

Sinha was looking guiltier by the second.

Juneja cocked an eyebrow at the cowering Sinha. 'Sajjan back?'

'No, sir.'

'No? So where is he? Still with Gupta?'

Sinha gave up trying to hedge. It was obvious—Fate was against him. Juneja was his liege. If Juneja wanted him to work, he'd have to, with or without Sajjan Kumar.

'Sir, Gupta Sir wants to move him to another police station, sir. There was a petition by the Mahila Mukti Andolan. Gupta Sir didn't want you to know, sir. His peon was telling me ...'

Ah, yes. The newest rape case on the block. If militant foreign women insisted on visiting sister organizations in short skirts, these things were bound to happen. What did they expect?

Theresa Schmidt was a member of some wretched German feminist outfit. What German women needed to be feminist about was beyond Juneja. A moot point. It was the men who needed help. The women were ten feet tall, had armpit hair that defied the imagination and a bristling moustache to boot *and* they spoke a language no one wanted to hear. *Well, the men speak it too, but that's beside the point.*

What was not a moot point was that Theresa Schmidt came to file an FIR because of some petty pilferage happening in the Mahila Mukti Andolan. She had chosen to do so at nine thirty at night, when, at least according to Sajjan Kumar, all respectable women are at home. She also chose to appear in a pair of cut-off jeans. Not that this fact had been bandied about, but Sinha had whispered it to Juneja meaningfully. Naturally, the sight of bristling legs had set Sajjan Kumar ablaze. He'd escorted her downstairs to the basement on the pretext of showing her some detainees. The basement had been empty and Sajjan's basket full.

It could all have been avoided. A little care, a little attention to detail. What happened after that was yet another moot point. One way of putting it was that Sajjan Kumar and Theresa Schmidt had had sex. Another was that she had three fractured ribs, a busted lip and some cuts here and there. Well, if the doctor was to be believed, mostly *there*; and now she was screaming rape. It's a moot point.

But it is a point to be made, Milord. Sajjan could be a tad harsh on the female sex.

Point taken. If you, Nikhil Juneja, are thinking about furthering you career, maybe you should do it without Sajjan Kumar.

'Find me the file that Gupta Sir gave on the road scam.'

Sinha handed it over quietly. The file looked thick. Untouched. Virginal. Unlike Theresa Schmidt. *Stupid cow, should have realized that even roads get raped here.*

Juneja sat back and inhaled deeply on the hot fag. Unlike earlier, the file made for interesting reading. A road scam wasn't quite the way he'd describe it, but well, it was about a road and a scam. Also, the entire thing was quite funny. In the village of Arse, a road was to be made. It was really called this, or rather, was spelt this way. The collator of the file made this specifically clear. It was to be pronounced Ur-sé. Like Ursa Major. The British had chosen to give the spelling a twist, claimed the erudite author of the report. *OK, whatever.*

In the village of Arse, a road was to be made. A noble intention. Considering the fact that there was little to put Arse on the map—no roads, no hospital, no nothing—it was, all told, a good idea. But the inhabitants of the village ... *what do you call inhabitants of Arse? Arseys? Arsians, perhaps? The report called them the* natives of Arse. *Hmm, maybe take turns.* The natives of Arse didn't think this was such a hot idea, although the government had offered compensation for the land. This was obviously a joke, but then the entire government has always been one and this couldn't have been entirely unknown to the Arseys, since, willy-nilly, they too were a part of the soon-to-be-twenty-first century. But the Arseys were not laughing at the governmental joke, especially since it was on them: the government was promising each villager Rs 50,000 as a one-time lump sum payoff for all small pieces of land. Medium and large pieces of land were strangely being given disproportionately more. They were also being offered a cut on the toll that would be levied on the stretch of road. But that was because they had such big pieces of land. By an even stranger quirk of fate, all the lower-caste members of Arse owned small pieces of land. The big landowners didn't. Juneja winced.

Fifty thousand as a one-time payoff? And after that a lifetime of slavery? Riddle me, riddle, riddle me this: what does an illiterate farmer with no skills for anything other than low-skilled farming do without land?

Bonded labour is an option. Suicide is another.

Hmm, cool choices.

Given the cool choices offered to them, the raw materials that had been delivered c/o Village Arse had been pilfered, stolen or had at least gone missing. This meant more delay.

Anyhow, the Arseys weren't having any of it; at least not the lower-caste Arseys. At this point, things got confusing for Juneja. There were a whole lot of castes mentioned. OBC and SC/ST in a column on a form is one thing, but this file here had names. Names of castes that Juneja didn't know had existed ... that they existed even in the soon-to-be-twenty-first century.

Well, Sajjan Kumar could probably help here.

Probably, Nikhil, probably, don't get your hopes up. Castes can't be fucked.

The caste-related distribution of land meant that, in effect, compensation was to be paid on the basis of caste. Although the report did not say so explicitly, once the

NGO brigade got hold of this, there would be hell to pay. No one may be discriminated against on the basis of caste, creed or colour.

Not your average scam, in other words. Neither government, nor vast sums of money involved. Was the leg-up also ruled out?

Quite clever of Gupta, thought Juneja, lighting another cigarette and choking. Bastard paan-wallah was selling fake Marlboro. Or Maar-boro as the cigarette said in fine print.

'Sinha,' bawled Juneja.

'Sir?'

'That bastard has given me fake cigarettes! Didn't you tell him who the cigarettes were for?'

'Sorry, sir.'

'Sorry,' grumbled Juneja, 'you want to kill me? This stuff is foul! Get me proper Marlboro Lights, OK? And tell the bastard, if he tries this again, I'll fix him and his mother and his nine sisters, OK?'

'Yes, sir,' said Sinha, grinning.

Somewhat mollified, Juneja tried another tack. 'Sinha, do you know anything about caste?'

'My caste, sir?'

'No, caste. In general, you know, caste.'

'Yes, sir! I am general category. Not SC/ST or OBC.'

'Right. Get out.'

So much for caste knowledge. It would have to be Sajjan Kumar, who had a fair chance of knowing something but was linguistically challenged. *Alternatively, I could ask Rajiv or maybe Geetu ... hmm.*

The long and the short of it was: compensation was to be paid on the basis of caste. However, the government claimed this was *not* the case. It was hardly the government's fault if the high-caste members of Arse owned more land than low-caste ones.

Oh yes, it is your fault, yelled the low Arseys right back. So and so many years ago, when the high Arseys grabbed our land, you didn't do anything about it.

Point to be noted, Milord.

High Arseys did not note it. In fact, they yelled objection right back.

Juneja didn't understand all this casteist stuff. But he understood completely when the government had sustained the objection.

Where would we be if some sweeper-type people could raise objections and get away with it? No, no, no … not now, not ever.

Sinha popped his head in. 'Sir, paan-wallah has no more Marlboro. Sir, Gold Flake alright? Old is gold!'

Another pearl of wisdom from Joseph's wretched progeny.

'Yes, fine, get Gold Flakes. Sajjan Kumar back?'

'Yes, sir. I have told him but he had to go to latrine.'

Sajjan Kumar came in at that moment.

'Do you have any cigarettes, Sajjan Kumar?'

'Yes, sir. Panama.'

'OK, give me one. Sinha, you go get the fags and get some tea or whatever. Are there any samosas left at the corner shop?'

'I will see, sir. How many?' asked Sinha, hopefully.

Juneja sighed. 'As many as you want. But not more than twenty, alright?'

Sinha beamed at his answer and sprinted off to get the samosas.

Juneja sat back with his Panama unfiltered. *God, slumming feels good.*

Sajjan Kumar wasn't looking too good.

Juneja knew he'd have to get his hands dirty. 'What happened with Gupta?'

'Not good, sir. They are demanding suspension.'

Juneja got up to go to the window. The sight in front did little to help solve the problem.

The bus stop was full with the usual, screaming load of maniacs, all intent on boarding this very bus. The buses belched smoke in their faces and threatened to leave without stopping. The people screamed, shoved and waged war. At times with their own person. If nothing else would stop the bus, they would hurl themselves in front of it. They would get killed, but others would be able to catch the bus. *In all this pushing and shoving, a little boob, a little ass, a little fondling never hurts anyone, does it?*

Delhi, the city of rapes. Every thirty minutes a woman got taken. Allegedly against her will. Juneja was taking nobody. Not even someone willing. Not that he wanted to either, of course. Sanjana had made some noises about being faithful. *Faithful. Faith-less is what being faithful is all about.*

He hadn't had a piece in months. Sanjana claimed she'd be able to tell if he did. Just by looking. This had petrified him into being celibate in her absence. His own wretched piece was ready to fall off. *Faithful. Stupid bloody word.*

Sinha came back in, startling Juneja out of his reverie with his silly crooning.

It was a strange scene: Sinha was holding a tray with three cups of tea and a paper bag containing the samosas. In his other hand were the cigarettes. With both hands full, he was unable to console Sajjan Kumar, who was crying silently. Sinha looked around wildly for a place to put down the tray. Juneja hastily put out the still-smouldering Panama and made some place on his overflowing table.

'No, no, Sajjan Kumar, you must not lose heart. There is nothing to worry about. Nothing to worry about.'

Juneja wasn't too sure about that.

'Well, Sajjan Kumar, let's talk things through and see what can be done.'

This suggestion made Sajjan Kumar weep even more, and this time noisily. 'Sir, sir, help me. What will happen to my children? To my wife? My mother? They all depend on me, sir. Who will marry my daughters, sir? I will be left nowhere, sir, help me!'

Anguished by this demand, Juneja grabbed the packet of cigarettes and lit up. But Sinha was up to the challenge. 'Don't be silly, Sajjan Kumar. Of course, Juneja Sir will help you. Old is gold and Juneja Sir is golden.'

The good thing about winter was the wonderful weather. In the summer, the water was hot, the air was hot, even the light you were forced to see was hot. Winter was cool: the air pleasant, the soft rays of the sun gently warmed the skin. There were few joys as satisfying as nodding off on a winter afternoon after a heavy lunch. Eat a fresh orange, crack a few peanuts. And then, slowly but surely, curl up under a thin blanket. Ideally, the blanket should be just a little small, so that some part of you was always left out. This meant curling up tight as a dog ... and slowly letting the sun do its work. During the course of the afternoon, the blanket would cease to be needed and cover just the feet. The waking hour would dawn as the sun lost its warmth. You are forced out of your sun-kissed slumber, softened and mellow, which in its way is nice… *But since it's Friday evening and not the bloody weekend, why not just stick to a bottle of rum?*

Sinha and Sajjan Kumar were preparing for the night shift. K. Joseph was officially on night shift and Sinha had managed to rig the roster so that he too could make an extra buck. Sajjan Kumar wanted to stay in the station to drink. Sinha was more than happy assisting him in this endeavour.

Joseph alone felt unhappy about their drinking on hallowed grounds, but was aware that there was little to be gained from objecting. Sajjan Kumar had been drinking every day for the past week. His local booze shop gave him a kickback, or a little present as he liked to call it. And ever since this rape scandal had broken out, he'd only been too happy to drink the present away.

Sajjan Kumar had sworn that he had done nothing to the woman. 'Joseph, you don't know these women. You know these Christian women … no, no, they're not people like Mary. Mary is my sister but they are foreign, these Christian women. They are on fire for Indian men. Just can't have enough. I told her no. No, I am a married man with six children. No, I have two daughters. Like flowers, like buds. Four boys, they are lions like their father.'

Here Sajjan Kumar broke off to shake his head sadly.

'I shouldn't have said anything to her about my children. I think that was the problem. You know, Joseph, *that* was the problem.'

'Why?'

'She was burning for me then. She thought, six children! Six, children! How virile, how manly he is! I must have him! And then she attacked me. Now, should I not defend myself, Joseph? You tell me!'

Joseph's wife Mary hadn't believed much of this story. They had had a whispered conversation after the children were safely in bed. Although her face had softened when Joseph told her that Sajjan Kumar considered her his sister, she had snorted contemptuously at his being attacked.

'Hah! Nothing, he just raped this woman! Stupid man!'

'How can you say that, Mary? Sajjan Kumar loves you very much. Even though we are Christians.'

'Yes, I love him too. But he is very stupid. This woman was also very stupid. When I came to Delhi as a little girl, I didn't know anything about Delhi. But my parents taught me. They learnt from their neighbours and they taught me. When you came from Kerala, you also knew nothing. How to behave, how to talk, where to go shopping, nothing you knew. But I showed you, didn't I?'

Joseph nodded. Mary had always supported him through thick and thin. She was a goddess. She was always right.

'But this woman, she comes here but knows nothing about us, our ways, our culture, our language, nothing. Then, this will happen! And whatever happens to Sajjan Kumar, whether he gets suspended or not, this woman has already been punished.'

Joseph was feeling quite punished as well. He'd happily have given up his night shift and passed it on to a very willing Sinha, but Juneja had said nothing doing.

The other policemen seemed to have no problem with the rape charges against Sajjan Kumar. Some had congratulated him about it, others had ignored it, yet others made censorious noises but continued to deal with Sajjan Kumar. Nobody felt the embarrassment that Joseph was anguished by. Sitting here as a teetotaller with Sajjan Kumar, drunk and bellicose, was terribly distressing. He found it even more unpleasant that Sinha seemed to think that it was completely the woman's fault.

'Silly whore,' he kept calling her.

It was only eleven o'clock and the shift had just started. It was going to be a long night.

Suddenly, there was a shout from the door. Startled, the trio looked up, but only Joseph was sober enough to make it to the door.

Eerie lights were burning at the entrance of the police station compound. They seemed to be surrounded: by lights, as well as a lack of noise. It was a curious hush. He could hear the unending sounds of traffic from the distant Ring Road. The heavy trucks were bringing in Delhi's daily food rations. But the sound merely served as a backdrop: like a black easel, where silence shines white.

The colleague who had called out looked wildly at Joseph. 'What is it? What should we do?'

'I don't know. Who are they?'

'I don't know either. They were just there. Suddenly.'

Joseph gulped, but evidently the lights meant no harm. At least not immediately.

He took the padlock and chain from the office and went to the entrance of the compound with the intention of putting on the chain.

They were women holding long, white candles. The kind that burnt in any household when the electricity breaks down. Almost all of them were dressed in white. White salwar kameezes, white saris, white shirts, white. But there was something else about them. Joseph jumped back, shocked.

It was their faces. They had painted their faces white. And on their faces were painted tears of blood.

One held a placard, 'Justice for Theresa Schmidt.'

Another came forward slowly. She too is holding a placard, thought Joseph. But it was a photograph. The woman's eyes met Joseph's as he stood amidst the alien throng, separated from them by the iron gate. She put down the photograph, propping it up against the compound gate, just inches away from where Joseph stood, unable to move, gripped by the silence.

'Joseph! Who is it?' yelled Sajjan Kumar from the police station. 'I've called up Juneja Sir. He'll be here as soon as possible.'

At the gate, nobody moved. Then another woman came forward and garlanded the photograph. The women came together, softly. Embracing each other, seeking solace at a police station that offered none.

Juneja did not, in fact, manage to arrive till almost three hours later. By that time not only was Gupta on the scene, but also several TV crews, journalists and sundry voyeurs who seemed bent on violence. The women remained silent. It was almost as if they had been waiting for Juneja.

He'd just entered the station from the side entrance when Gupta accosted him. 'Arre, Juneja, what the hell, man! Where are you? Is this any time to appear? Sajjan Kumar is hiding in the basement, TV journalists are here and you are happily sleeping?'

Chastened, Juneja studied his feet. 'Sir, I'm sorry. My mobile was switched off and—'

'I don't want to hear about your bloody mobile! Get out over there and talk to these bloody people! What nonsense is this? Now that this cell phone nonsense has started, you duffers are even more difficult to locate! Now do I have to get down on my knees to get you to find out what these vultures want or will you finally do the job that you are paid for?'

Since there did not appear to be any possible rejoinder to this, Juneja did precisely that.

The waiting carrion attacked at once. It was like a maelstrom of light, flashes and questions. He caught single words but couldn't understand a question.

'Action!'

'Police brutality!'

'Say!'

'Answer!'

How? Bemused, Juneja raised a hand to ask for silence. It was abruptly granted. But before Juneja could open his mouth, one of the painted ladies of the night stepped forward. She wore a plain white sari. She stood in front of the locked gates of the police station compound and effectively blocked out Juneja.

'We are not members of any political organization, nor are we here to attack or harm anybody. The padlock on this gate is a sign of the insecurity of the police.'

She paused meaningfully before continuing in a low, serious tone that got on Juneja's nerves. She almost certainly wore only jute and khadi. *Bitch.* And definitely no deodorant. He could smell the acrid whiff of sincerity.

'To police a country is no easy job. But to take advantage of the position of the guard and to steal the treasure within is the worst kind of treachery. It is a heinous act.'

Good god, woman! Get a life! It was just a horny act. Don't act like it's never happened before. Or maybe it hasn't happened to you. Better start wearing deodorant!

'At nine o'clock in the evening today, Theresa Schmidt's body was found. She committed suicide with an overdose of the sleeping tablets that had been prescribed to her after the rape. We don't call it suicide. We call it murder. Sajjan Kumar did not just rape Theresa Schmidt. He has abused every woman ... abused the sacred trust placed on him as a policeman. He has killed the faith of every woman in Delhi, who no longer feels safe—on the streets, in her office, in her very home.'

Do you ever feel safe on the streets of Delhi? How? Why?

'We demand that Sajjan Kumar be suspended immediately. We demand a fair and extensive investigation of the case. We demand an apology from the Delhi Police. Till our demands are met, we will conduct a twenty-four-hour serial vigil in front of the Basantpur police station.'

Serial vigil? Now, there's a killer. Well, nothing more to say to that. Juneja walked back in, wondering what they could possibly do now.

Inside was Chaos Central. Gupta was screaming incoherently at a constable. All the phones were ringing or being hollered into. Police personnel ran around like headless chickens, mostly, suspected Juneja, to look busy and stay out of Gupta's way, who was looking fit to murder. The villain of the piece, Sajjan Kumar, was nowhere to be seen. Gupta had said that he was lurking in the basement.

But, wait a minute, where the hell is Sinha? And that cockeyed bastard Joseph has disappeared as well.

'So Juneja, what is your bright idea now? This fool, Sajjan Kumar, has really overdone it! Where is he?'

'Sir, I will find him immediately and come to your room.' *Clever and discreet. The old bugger should stop screaming in the corridor.*

'No! If I go over to the annexe and that too with that fool, all hell will break loose. Arre! We will sit in your office.'

'Yes, sir, of course. I'll get some tea organized.'

Gupta stomped off, looking temporarily mollified.

The moment the door shut behind him, there was a palpable drop in tension, which Juneja immediately hiked up by glaring at some scurrying minion. 'Make some tea. Now! And hurry up.'

In the basement were the old dungeons of Castle Basantpur. Juneja looked around, picking his way gingerly through what looked like nuclear refuse. At the far end, a light was still burning.

Sajjan Kumar sat flanked by Joseph and Sinha. Obviously, Joseph was the only one sober. Sinha was swaying and Sajjan Kumar looked like he was on the verge of passing out.

'What the hell are you doing here?'

A deflated Joseph, looking exhausted, answered sadly, 'Sir, I brought them down here. If Gupta Sir sees them like this, then—'

The fool was right. On the other hand, if he didn't get Sajjan Kumar up there fast, his ass was going to fry.

'Get him cleaned up. No, Joseph,' he cut off any opposition, 'I don't care how you do it. Just do it. Make him throw up or something, anything, alright? This fool Sinha should just go home. He is not going to get any pay for today and tell him I want to see him first thing he reports tomorrow. Is that clear?'

It was amply clear and Joseph had understood.

'Sir?' It was a desperate whisper. Juneja barely heard it. He wanted to get out of this smelly hellhole as fast as possible.

He turned with one foot already on the step. Joseph came to him at a run.

'Sir, have those women gone?'

Juneja closed his eyes in irritation.

'Joseph, don't be silly. You think Gupta has come here to kiss Sajjan Kumar goodnight or what? Obviously they haven't gone. In fact, they've brought journalists, TV cameras and a shitload of trouble with them. Now, is there anything else I can do for you or may I leave?'

Juneja's voice had been rising steadily much to Joseph's dismay, who made urgent hushing movements with his hand.

'What is it?'

'Sir, you know Sajjan Kumar is a little under the influence of alcoholic spirits—'

'He's dead bloody drunk, yes.'

'Sir, sir, before that he told me, sir, he confessed, sir, he has done it.' Joseph's voice was barely a whisper. 'The women are right. Sir, he has raped her. Now what will we do?'

2 October 1999

It was damn near seven o'clock in the morning by the time Juneja got home. It had proven impossible to get Sajjan Kumar sober and he had, after an unnecessarily long time, simply passed out.

Juneja's genius had prompted him to call an ambulance from the hospital to carry Sajjan Kumar away. Later, the police would release a statement saying some rubbish about a heart problem. Palpitation sort of stuff. Nothing anyone could do anything about.

It was the only way. Gupta had been apoplectic and would probably have kicked Sajjan Kumar to death. Sinha too was in danger of a departmental inquiry into his drunken behaviour. He'd managed to salvage the situation somewhat by putting all the blame on Sajjan Kumar, who'd been too comatose to deny anything.

Joseph, of course, had come out of the entire thing smelling of roses. And much to Juneja's barely concealed satisfaction, also of Sinha's vomit. All told, it had not been a good night for Team Juneja.

At home, Diwan Singh, his trusted retainer, was looking fresh as a daisy. Juneja told him that he was going back to bed and should not be awoken under any circumstances.

Diwan Singh smirked, 'And the morning pooja?

'Pooja? Have you gone mad? I haven't done bloody pooja in forty years and I'm not starting now! Are you mad or, or, or drunk?'

The last was a spur-of-the-moment insult. Diwan Singh was going through a deeply religious phase. Of late, he'd taken to watching religious channels with a passion and the query was sure to enrage him.

Diwan Singh kept his calm, albeit with some effort. The damned holy channels seemed to be having some effect.

He mastered his face, which had been threatening to scowl, and put on a deceptively benign look. 'No, I am very much sober, as indeed I always am.' The benevolence became slightly vicious at the edges. 'But you will recollect that today is the *naamkaran* of Rajiv's daughters.'

Juneja struggled with his own features but there was no way he could keep his calm. 'What the hell do you mean? It's next week!'

'No.'

And the bastard made to turn around.

'Where are you going?'

And this time there was no hiding the smirk. 'To make you tea. I'm sure you'll be fresh and ready to leave after a shower.'

'Diwan Singh, have you gone mad?'

Juneja knew that he was being kept dangling because of the wretched crack about being drunk. He always ended up paying. The man finally took pity.

'Rajiv called up early this morning—'

'How early? It's only seven thirty now!'

'Yes, but they are having some problems with their pundit. He may not be able to come because he is not well.'

'And so he called me up? I'm a policeman, not a bloody priest!' Juneja sank down in a chair, feeling limp with relief. Hopefully, the bloody priest was dead and the wretched ceremony would be postponed or whatever.

'No, he called me. That's why he called here at six o'clock. He wanted me to find out about a replacement pundit.'

Juneja rode out the waves of revulsion. 'And did you?'

'In two minutes flat. I wanted Pundit Hari Maharajji but he had a prior appointment. Then he called me back and said his appointment had been cancelled and that he would be free. So he will be coming to Rajiv's house at ten o'clock,' concluded Diwan Singh.

There was no possible escape and the entire wretched affair was going to be dull as ditchwater.

He breathed in deeply. Two and a half hours to go. There was no question of going to sleep. He'd only feel worse.

'OK, forget the tea. I'll make coffee when I get out of the shower. I want breakfast.'

'Eggs?'

'And meat. Make kebabs or something. And lots of them, alright?'

Diwan Singh nodded dourly. He knew Juneja's methods.

Juneja dragged himself to the bathroom, shedding his smelly clothes as he went. They stank of exhaustion, sweat and Sajjan Kumar. *Asshole. It was all because of him.*

Thankfully, Diwan Singh had put on the geyser early in the morning. The water was steaming hot and Juneja made the most of it. The ceremony was going to be a killer. All of Rajiv's horrible, yodelling female relatives would be there. To top it, Geetu's clan would also be present. And they made Rajiv's lot look like a bunch of drunk monkeys.

'Actually, it's a function concerning the womenfolk, mainly,' Rajiv had confided.

Juneja could feel his balls cringe. *Why? Why call it a function? And why call the harpies womenfolk?*

'So what the fuck are we going to do there?'

'Don't be crazy, man, Nikhil! I'm the father. *Obviously* I have to be there!'

But I'm not the bloody father. Juneja desisted from saying it. Somehow.

'And what should I do there?'

'Man, Nikhil, if I have just the relatives I'll go mad, man.'

Juneja nodded sadly. It was true. He'd go mad himself.

'OK, but what do you want me to do?'

'Man, Nikhil, you know, just like take the stuff from me ... I mean the envelopes that people will give ... and you know, if you could just keep an eye on the food and drink arrangements—'

'At the bar?'

And Rajiv had had the temerity to laugh. 'Man, Nikhil, you're really funny! It's only fruit juice and lassi. And no meat, man, it's not allowed. And Nikhil, Geetu asked me to ask you something.'

Rajiv paused and then asked Juneja's shoes, 'Could you please not smoke in front of everyone? You know, respect and all.'

No meat, no bar and no cigarettes. In other words, no food, no drink, no fun. This was the whole problem with adopting children.

Despite the uneasiness between them, Diwan Singh was a pearl beyond price. Not that Juneja would ever think of telling him this.

Diwan Singh had laid out an outfit he considered right for the festivities. Juneja found it hideous and couldn't, in fact, remember ever buying it. It was an outfit destined to make a peacock envious. Startling green kurta, blue pajama and a wretched stole that combined both colours.

The entire ensemble shimmered and glittered, or was he just knackered beyond belief? He picked it up. *Yoicks!* It was some strange kind of plasticky crepe.

Where the hell did this come from? 'Diwan Singh!'

Juneja and Diwan Singh had been at loggerheads for some time now. Diwan Singh was almost certainly always watching the newest devotional channels, which telecast live *jagraatas*. And thanks to the festive season, there were any number of them happening. Since Diwan Singh insisted on hearing them at top volume, Juneja had finally bought him a pair of headphones. Diwan Singh had been enraged by this purchase and had since made it a point to wear them all the time.

Time again to go into the holiest of the holies? Juneja was sick of it. 'Diwan Singh?' he knocked on the door.

The door was opened reluctantly. Diwan was a sight to behold. He was immaculately dressed as usual. His hair was standing on end from the hastily ripped-off headphones, which lay on the ground. The TV screen was silently full of maddened devotees.

Juneja shook his head.

'It is the jagraata from yesterday. The devotees are possessed with the spirit of Ma,' Diwan Singh offered as an answer.

'No more live telecast?'

'It ended last night … at two o'clock. I couldn't watch it since I had to get up early today … because of the pooja. The channel repeats the shows throughout the day,' but of course live is best, his tone implied. It was Juneja's fault that he had to watch a rerun.

'So it's my fault?'

'Do you think it's your fault? Did I say that?'

'No. You didn't. Never mind. What are these clothes?'

'The ones on your bed? Rajiv sent them.'

'What?'

'You can call him, but he told me to get them ready for you because, today, you are part of the family and he wants you to be dressed in the same colours.'

A colour-coordinated pooja?

There was only one answer. 'Have you got the kebabs ready?'

Stuffed to the gills with meat, Juneja finally went to change. Thank god for Indian clothes. The drawstring pajama always accommodated a paunch. After the entire wretched thing was on, he sneaked a look in the mirror. *Ye Gads!* It was worse than he'd ever thought possible. Bastard Rajiv had got him a kurta a size too small, so that instead of falling like a waterfall, the garment coyly clung to his curves. In profile, he looked six months pregnant. OK, maybe four, if the light was flattering. The ghastly shimmer made his pate glow. Maybe he should buy some foundation or something to give it a matt finish? It had a tendency to sweat ...

He carefully avoided looking at Diwan Singh, who was looking natty in crisp whites. 'Are we leaving immediately?'

'Yes, Rajiv asked if we could be early. He wants you to help receive guests and I'm needed in the kitchen.'

The flaming colour of the car made Juneja wince some more. They'd look like a psittacine procession. But thankfully the way was short. Nobody would have the time to recognize him. Even if they did, he'd just lie and say it wasn't him. Sanjana was really the only person who mattered and, hopefully, America was too far to see the glitter. At the crossing in front of the house, he almost crashed the car. His father! His father would be there!

Rajiv's sense of duty would make him invite Juneja Sr. who, of course, would come. After all why should he forego the opportunity to see his son dressed like a designer clown in public?

The entire house was decked out in marigold and roses. Not too many people had come as yet, but Rajiv's servant took the car to park it far away, so that other guests would have more parking space closer to the house. Juneja went off in search of Rajiv.

Rajiv? Nope, Rajiv Senior, also ashimmer in green and blue.

'Namaste, Uncle!' Juneja made the ubiquitous half-dive towards his feet and ended up grazing his paunch. He also discovered anew that the kurta was tight beyond belief.

'Hello, my son, hello! Yes, hello, hello!' Rajiv's father tended to be hearty when embarrassed. Who wouldn't be? Dressed like a hopefully-soon-to-be-extinct parrot species? Juneja took the opportunity to suck in his breath so that the kurta could fall past his paunch.

They were smiling sadly at each other when Rajiv's mother came in. Juneja immediately dove for her feet. It was either that or he was passing out. She was dressed in glittering orange and yellow. But he remembered to suck in his breath beforehand.

'Uncle, these colours ... Is this something patriotic?'

'No, beta.' Uncle was pained beyond belief. 'It's just a colour scheme that Geetu thought would be appropriate. You know the ladies like the marigolds, the men like the rose leaves and the children—'

'Are the roses,' finished Juneja. *Change the bloody subject, Nikhil, now, do it* now!

'So, what names have been chosen? Rajiv wouldn't tell me.'

Uncle was now looking as if the boil on his ass was about to be lanced. 'Beta, that is a state secret. Geetu, you know—'

Juneja nodded. Indeed, who didn't know iron-balled Geetu? Considering her potency, Juneja was surprised she hadn't managed to inseminate herself. Why bother to adopt?

'But, Uncle, where is Geetu?'

'Beta, she and Rajiv and the girls have gone to the temple. Geetu and Rajiv believe this is a new phase of their married life, as parents.'

Does that mean Geetu will never put out again? Poor Rajiv!

Uncle continued, 'They have gone to seek the blessings of Bhole Nath, the most exemplary of fathers.'

Juneja blinked at that one. Hadn't Shiva cut off his son Ganesh's head? *Well, it was an example of sorts.*

As the morning progressed, Juneja felt himself falling into rituals and traditions with an ease he hadn't thought possible. Although he was, strictly speaking, a Sikh, Delhi—the great leveller after death and taxes—had made him a mongrel. He was able to speak pidgin Punjabi, not understood in Punjab, bastardized Hindi, not understood in UP, and Indian English, not understood outside the country—he had become a Delhiite. In addition to all this, he'd also picked up a smattering of Hindu rituals—Vaishno Devi, karva chauth, the wretched jagraatas Diwan Singh was so fond of, and naturally the naamkaran, the naming ceremony.

Rajiv and Geetu made a grand entrance at about eleven thirty. Rajiv too was parroting around. Geetu was in an even more resplendent version of the orange garb that Rajiv's mother was decked out in. Luckily, the naming ceremony concerned women only. Juneja took the opportunity to have a quick fag in the bathroom.

After that it was non-stop action. People had started pouring in and Juneja was hard-pressed keeping all the money-envelopes that were forced into Rajiv and Geetu's supposedly unwilling hands.

'Just a token!'

He'd been given the keys to the bedroom and had already made two trips to put away all the loot. The girls, who to Juneja's critical eye were coal black, had been given the names Swantika and Dhwani. Juneja found himself muttering Swunny and Dhwunny obsessively. He forced himself to stop and then discovered that he had started mouthing inanities about Swantika and Dhwantika being lovely names.

By the time lunch was in full flow, so was Juneja. It was easy to conduct conversations about which airport was the best (Changi) and which airline the most comfortable (Thai). Sexiest air hostesses, Singapore, worst, Air India. It was the kind of conversation he'd had with an infinite number of men he didn't know and would never meet again. Nonetheless, in the here and now it was the kind of mindless conversation he could repeat ad nauseam. If they'd had access to alcohol, the conversation would have slowly moved via non-vegetarian jokes to the Reeperbahn. It was similar to the airport version. Delhi's local G.B. Road was to be derided. If you were really the hot and rich and self-confident type, you said something about a blonde head bobbing down there in San Francisco and of course you'd seen her smoke and snake in Patpong. There must be a female version of this kind of social claptrap. Juneja suspected it had to do with 'you really can't get any decent domestic help nowadays…'. There was the further variation of 'my mother-in-law … what a bitch she was' but that was the same as the servant diatribe.

So how was that so different from the male chatter? It was all about a price/performance ratio. Airports, sex and servants. Same difference.

Juneja was happy flitting from group to group, making sure everyone went to eat. At the back of his mind, he kept seeing images of his own uncles, his father, the endless dos of the past, the easy chatter. It was like being in a time machine. The old groove, well worn and smooth.

He got various old biddies dessert. He made sure that people went for seconds. He filled glasses and pushed the waiters around to the right people. He checked on Geetu's foul relatives and made sure that strange faces had someone to talk to.

In general, he acted like a presidential candidate. Gentle flirting with the women, macho joviality with their husbands, respectful deference with the fogeys and diffident head patting with the kids. *Just as well.*

Rajiv certainly wasn't playing the attentive host. He was drunk on parenthood. He and Geetu seemed unable to do anything but grin, and Juneja suspected that this newest obsession with progeny was going to be the death knell for their relationship.

A husky voice broke into his reverie.

'Looking very handsome today, Nikhil.'

Juneja drew in a deep breath. His father was a tough customer and it would be insane to risk having a scene here. Someone, somewhere would be avariciously taking in the gossip. Like Rajiv's parents, who knew all about The Rift. Well, not the exact reasons, but that they were estranged. He swallowed his pride and made a shallow dive.

C'mon Nikhil, play to the gallery!

Since his father was more or less concave, there was no paunch to stop him freefalling. He found himself more or less on level with his father's knees before his father grabbed his shoulder and pulled him upright. His kurta gave a warning creak.

'Filial love, Nikhil?' It was a bemused question, but his father didn't wait for an answer. 'I have spoken to your senior … Gupta. Nikhil, your grandmother has been keeping very ill. I would like to take her out of Delhi for the winter. You know she has a very difficult time with the smog and the cold. It would be a good time for you to get initiated into the business. You could do it without me breathing over your shoulder.' The last was said with a distinctly sardonic smile.

'Is that why you contacted Gupta?'

'Nikhil, Gupta's father is an old associate of your grandfather. These people go back to before Partition. We keep in touch for any number of reasons. One being that you are in the police.'

The Holy Partition. The Great Big Indian Show. The gobstopper to stop all gobs.

Correctly interpreting Juneja's silence as sullen, his father continued, 'Nikhil, give me an answer. The business is huge and it would be a pity if all that I have worked for were to go after my death. But if you are happy in the police, I have to respect your decision and then ...' His father floundered.

'Then?'

'Then, Nikhil, that is that. A large sum of money, property, etc. will in any case come to you after my death. But if your decision is irrevocable and you are definitely not interested, I will start winding down the business and liquidating assets rather than making long-term investments.'

Decisions, decisions.

'Why do I have to do this now?' It was a cry from the heart and judging by the smarmy smile on his father's face, he recognized it as such.

'Nikhil, you're forty-five. Not twenty-five. In another five years you will be fifty.'

'I can do the math.'

'I'm sure you can. Can you also learn and adapt at any age? How long do you want to wait before getting married, settling down, having children? Your grandmother is reconciled to dying before seeing a great-grandchild. Do

I have to do the same? Or will you invite me to a circus similar to this one at the end of it?'

Although his father's voice hadn't risen, Juneja knew they were a microsecond away from full-scale war.

'Give me an answer, Nikhil. As far as I'm concerned it doesn't have to be today. But we don't have endless amounts of time. I have watched you wasting your time for fifteen years. Surely even you must be tired of the entire affair by now.'

'What affair?' Did his father suspect something?

'I don't know, Nikhil, and quite frankly I don't want to know. I don't know why you wanted to join the wretched police force and why we had to go through this nonsense. Write a book about it at some point and tell me, alright? I'll read it after my retirement ... If Diwan Singh is to be believed, there is a young lady you are interested in. Oh! Stop scowling, he's loyal to you but the man can have some loyalty to me as well, can't he? After all, who pays his wages?'

Juneja couldn't bring himself to speak.

His father controlled himself with obvious difficulty, pasted a smile on his face and continued through clenched teeth: 'If Diwan Singh is to be believed, you have been seeing a young lady for some time now. If this is serious, if you are serious about her, then I suggest you also get serious about life and give me an answer. Preferably, as soon as possible.'

Juneja looked away. *As soon as bloody possible.*

He felt the soft vibration of his cell phone against his

thigh before its clamorous demands made themselves heard. He smiled warmly at his father. 'Do excuse me, I must take this call.'

The manna from heaven rapidly disintegrated into white and green bird shit. It was Gupta, squawking about a wretched emergency. Would Juneja kindly come over to the police station?

When?

Oh, about an hour *ago* would be good. Failing that, now, immediately, asap.

Juneja made some ineffective noises—which failed to soothe Gupta—and hung up. He went off to Rajiv to bid farewell only to realize that he, Juneja, would not fare so well without a steed, i.e., a car. He then ran around looking for the wretched servant who had parked the car. This obviously proved to be impossible. He called up Gupta again to say that it would take a little longer since he was at a … well, a function and currently without transport. Gupta informed him, rather brusquely, that a car would be sent for him.

Juneja immediately felt better. Quite a few other guests were leaving and Juneja knew they would all see him climbing into the police jeep looking suave and manly … despite the party dress.

Hopefully, it would be a jeep with a few thugs carrying AK-47s.

Not very likely.

Still, one never knows.

Juneja stood outside the house and lit up. Now that all the uncles and aunties were inside, he could smoke in peace.

Also, there were some PYTs standing around. Maybe they would hit on him … especially when the police car came and the thugs saluted. Women always, *always* dug men in uniform. Juneja could never understand it. Not that he wasn't grateful for it but still the crap khaki? Who gets their rocks off on a colour like that?

The police jeep came with the blue alarm on. Juneja smirked and strode up to it in a manly way. Joseph was in the car, looking more like a rat than ever. Juneja glared at him and hauled himself in.

'Good afternoon, sir! Sorry to interrupt your function. Gupta Sir has said full speed. Major emergency, sir.'

Idiot.

'Afternoon.'

Somewhat deflated, Joseph tried again. 'Looking very handsome, sir! Family function?'

Juneja refused to rise to the bait. He gave Joseph a glacial stare as his mind went into feverish overdrive. Was he really on his way to the police station in parrot gear? Gupta would have his guts for garters.

As it turned out, it wasn't Gupta who wanted Juneja-brand garters—it was the wretched press. The bloody women were still serial protesting in front of the station. Innumerable journalists and cameras formed a seething mass around them. Juneja cowered inside the jeep trying to hide, but to little avail. The blood suckers swarmed around the vehicle, shooting questions and flashbulbs in his face at the same time. Juneja shielded his eyes with one hand and hoped to render himself unrecognizable.

As a ploy, it didn't work. The next day would show him looking not unlike a shy bride—a singularly unflattering image printed in colour in the Delhi supplement of a leading newspaper.

Juneja wanted the jeep to bring him to the very doorstep in order to avoid further photo ops. This tactic too was destined to fail. The gates had to be opened inch-wise to let only his vehicle through. The process necessarily entailed delay and Juneja found himself stranded amidst the hostile crowd.

'Welcome, Nikhil, welcome! I hope we are not inconveniencing you, hmm? Distracting you from your hectic social life? Thank you for dropping in. Why should you bother wearing a uniform, hmm? Arre! I hope the press got your best profile?'

Juneja maintained a politic silence. Gupta was always sarcastic in the beginning. If you tried to reason with him at this stage, things would get out of hand. Better to let him have his fifty paise of flesh. The only irritating thing was that it was happening in front of all the others. Gupta was lampooning him in public and he, Nikhil Juneja, had to take it ... in and because of the damned parrot costume.

'Sir, I was not aware of the emergency and was thus unable to change into my uniform.' *Thus? Are you becoming Joseph? Who talks thus in real life? Are you also going to say thereafter or, better still, hereafter?*

Gupta smouldered nastily at him some more before marching off into his office. His, Juneja's office. Evidently, after last evening's fracas, Gupta had taken over his office.

Juneja gave it a minute or two before going in, which was hard, because the men milling about him were so *not* looking at him.

Obviously, it would have been too much to expect Gupta to sit in a visitor's chair. Even so, Juneja was taken aback at the ease with which his entire office had been appropriated. Gupta seemed to be entirely at home. He was yapping with his missus on his cell phone *and* had his feet up on the table. He waved airily at Juneja, indicating a seat.

Juneja was happy to oblige. He sat down for the first time in a long day, only to straighten up stiffly. In fact, extremely stiffly. The kurta was unexpectedly tight around the stomach and needed to be slyly adjusted without too much pulling … *yes, that is the way, slowly, inch by inch, the cloth will let you breathe …*

'Nikhil?'

Juneja jumped out of his skin and the kurta ripped. Thankfully not audibly, but he was going to have to leave the office backwards like an out-of-grace courtier in a Mughal court, arms pasted to his ripped sides.

'Is everything alright? You're looking very sad. Nikhil, are you OK?'

'Yes, sir. My father told me today that my grandmother has been keeping unwell,' Juneja said, allowing his voice to break ever so slightly.

Gupta did a manful quiver of his own. Ah, the Grandmother of the Partition! But the sorrow of it all didn't deter him any.

'Nikhil, I have been talking to my superiors. We will

have to institute an inquiry into the Sajjan Kumar/Theresa Schmidt case.'

Ye gads! Is this what it is being called? The Sajjan Kumar/ Theresa Schmidt Case? Being a Case was the first step on the road to professional disaster. *Poor Sajjan Kumar is doomed ...*

'How can I help, sir?' Juneja to the forefront. After all, what was the point sticking his neck out for Sajjan Kumar? Bastard hadn't known when or where to stick his dick; he could hardly expect Juneja to take the rap for him.

'I know, Nikhil, and your commitment to duty makes me proud of you.'

Like hell! You would sell me out at the drop of a hat, you old fart!

And then the old fart did.

'But, Nikhil, there is too much pressure on me, and on the department right now.' Gupta showed him a press clipping.

It was some bastard journalist who had had the temerity to ask for an investigation against Juneja on moral grounds.

> Was Sajjan Kumar not a trusted assistant
> of ACP Juneja?

Bastard. Haemorrhoidal bastard.

'Nikhil, I think the best thing is for you to take up the road scam case. I told you, this is a case better managed without Sajjan Kumar. Take another junior officer and leave.'

'But, sir, I mean, my grandmother—'

'No, Nikhil, I want you to leave for this village as soon as possible. I will let you know when things have settled down here. In fact, you will come back yourself. Ablaze, charging in on your white stallion of victory, bringing glory to our name, and tears to the eyes of your grandmother!'

Juneja's best excuses, including dragging in the Holy Grandmother, were in vain. Gupta said that in this day of mobile phones, Juneja would be able to stay in touch with his grandma. Besides, what would happen to G-Ma's dicky heart if little Nikki landed up under an investigation? Hmm? No, no, no. Besides, Arse wasn't all that far from Delhi. A mere three hours' drive. More or less equidistant from Miraat on the one side and Pankot on the other. It would be like a holiday. A colonial times-style holiday. Really. Gupta suggested he take someone, hmmm, Joseph? with him. But at least *this* brilliant idea Juneja was able to quash ruthlessly. A holiday with Joseph? Even Gupta wouldn't want that. Besides, what would happen to Sajjan Kumar without Joseph?

Gupta had agreed sadly. Nobody else was stupid enough to volunteer to take care of Sajjan Kumar, whose star was clearly on the descent. The job could only be palmed off on Joseph, who had no star to speak of. Sajjan Kumar—drunk, raping and raging—was more than most people could bear.

So who would accompany Juneja? 'Nobody' was so far the only answer Juneja could come up with. For the time being, Gupta agreed. Juneja would sod off to Arse and report after three or four days. Reservations would be made at some bloody government guest house. The local police station wasn't local since it was in Miraat. But they had also been instructed to offer full cooperation to Juneja. *Bastards.*

After that, there really wasn't much to discuss with Gupta. And Juneja backed off in a hurriedly summoned taxi with the distinct feeling that Gupta wasn't expecting him back. Otherwise, why appropriate his office like this?

Juneja paid off the taxi at the local paan-wallah and picked up three cartons of cigarettes as supplies. What else would he need for the wilderness? Booze? Well, a couple of bottles certainly wouldn't hurt. It was unlikely that there would be no booze shop in the wilderness. Wilderness always meant that even if you got no food, you got alcohol. Usually moonshine, which was probably the only way you could bear to screw the local flesh. But perhaps a bottle of something good, a single malt of some kind?

Gupta had told him that the people in Miraat would expect him on Monday, which meant that a boozy weekend could easily be enjoyed. He decided to go home and check on the existing stock of booze at home and then think about the rest.

First things first, get the car back. Only assholes walk.

He pulled out his cell phone and called Rajiv. 'Hi, man! What's the scene like?'

'Hang on, Nikhil, just hang on a second. I need to get to a place where I can hear you.'

Rajiv was evidently in the midst of a huge party. Juneja could hear Daler Mehendi belting out his stuff.

Rub, rub, tub, tub or is it love, love?

'Man, where did you disappear? It's swinging over here! Get your ass back over here!'

'Are you serious? Man, I thought this was a children's party.'

'Sure, it was! The older children are partying now!'

Sounded good.

'Great! Rajiv, my car is over at your place. I think this new servant of yours parked it somewhere. Can you get him to pick me up?'

'A new servant? Man, Nikhil you know all the guys. Who d'you mean? Geetu, wait a minute I'm just getting back, Nikhil sorry, it's madness here.'

'Man, I don't know the fucker's name. Some flunky who was parking the cars. A valet in, I think, a white outfit?'

'Valet? The guy who was parking the cars? Gagan?'

'Yeah, I think that was his name. Just have him drive over and pick me up. I'll just have a quick shower and be ready by the time he arrives. Fucker was nowhere to be found when I left. You should keep your servants under more control, man!'

'He's Geetu's brother.'

Hmm, it is *hard to speak, when your socks are in your molars.* Juneja could feel the frost creep right up to where he was standing.

'Sorry, man, I just didn't realize, so just send Diwan Singh with the car? Assuming you still want me at your party after I've insulted your brother-in-law?'

'Sure, man, no problem, one chauffeur coming right up!'

'Bye!'

At home, the lights were still off, which meant that he could strip and stuff the parrot outfit into a plastic bag—to be thrown before Diwan Singh saw it or, worse still, had it repaired. He'd just finished putting on a pair of jeans and a clean white shirt when the bell rang.

He opened the door to the same valet parking asshole, who also was now dressed as a parrot.

'Hello, sir! I'm Gagan. Geetu didi is my sister.'

Gross asshole. Village life looked better and better.

'Hi, Gagan! Please do call me Nikhil. Your brother-in-law and I went to school together. Would you like to come in? Have a drink? I just need to put on some shoes and we can go.'

'Please, sir, I mean Nikhil Sir, no formalities. Jiju, I mean, Rajiv, has often told me about you. Just water is fine.'

'Water? You can have a whisky. I won't tell Geetu!'

'No, sir, I mean Nikhil Sir, I, I don't take hard drinks.'

Juneja waved him in the direction of a chair and went off in search of appropriate footwear and not-so-hard water. Thanks to Gagan's perfect timing, he wouldn't have time for a quick one either.

So Rajiv has been telling you about me? I'll bet he has. Has he told you about how we wanked over Playboy? *Or how your stupid sister doesn't give him enough? Or how the newest* Hustler *is always hidden behind the cistern of the guest bathroom? Hmm? Has he?*

Gagan maintained a polite flow of chit-chat all the way to the house. How wonderful his, Juneja's, car was. And red was a great colour. He was personally thinking of buying a car as well. Turned out the fucker came from some small town type of place where he lived with his parents. Who else? No chick in her right mind would want to shack up with him. He was twenty-four. *Twenty bloody four.* Geetu was his older, much revered sister. He was planning on coming to Delhi for further studies. *Right.* He was the kind of guy who would study further. Study your sister a little further, bro!

The house was still ablaze with lights, but it was the deafening music around the house that reassured Juneja. The older children were indeed at play.

It had started out well enough. The music had been assaulting his ears even before they entered—always a very good or a very bad sign. An extreme sign. Inside, the scene defied the imagination. Rajiv had said something about older children partying, by which Juneja had understood himself and others of his ilk. Not the geriatric ward of the All India Institute of Medical Sciences. Rajiv's parents, Geetu's parents, aunts and uncles, and various others in their dotage could evidently not get enough of the groove. The dance floor was a seething mass of diamonds, grey foliage and wrinkled, droopy flesh. The cool young chicks were sitting on the sides, cheering on the (much) older generation. Rajiv, not content with the amount of heaving, undulating walking sticks on the floor, was working the crowd, imploring grannies and grandpas to jive.

Juneja turned to the transfixed Gagan by his side. 'I didn't realize what a funky family Geetu had!'

Gagan was wobbling his head to the beat, trying in vain to keep up with his jiving parents. 'They love Daler Mehendi; he's just too good.'

'Yeah, he's my dad's favourite too.' *Yes, Nikhil, remember your* father*'s favourite, not* yours.

If the party was going to continue on these lines, he might as well leave for Arse immediately. Plus, he was feeling shattered because of the lack of sleep. Among other things.

'Hi, Nikhil, man, there you are! Gagan got you over? Good. Nothing like a trustworthy driver, hmm?'

'Yes, Rajiv.' Juneja tried not to sound quite so discomfited, but Rajiv appeared not to have told Gagan.

'Great party. Really floor thumping. Have you got a DJ?'

'Naturally, man, he's just gone to the loo, so I was having a spin. But first let me get you a drink. What'll you have?'

Juneja felt his clenched buttocks relax. It wasn't going to be all that bad. 'Vod—'

'There's lassi and juice. Also, Geetu's dad has mixed some fresh thandai.'

'Thandai? With bhang?' Juneja tried to keep his voice low. *Geetu's dad dabbled in drugs?*

'No, Nikhil, obviously not. *Veg* thandai, really good with fresh almonds.'

'I'll have a juice.'

'I'll get it, Jiju,' Gagan offered. 'Apple, sir ... or orange? We've got it fresh from Himachal. So I can really recommend the apple. It's my favourite.'

'I'll have orange. Apple gives me flatulence.'

Not very sure of the meaning, Gagan tried to put on an understanding smile and went off to the juice bar.

'Seriously, Rajiv, great party.'

'You know, Nikhil, you've got to get settled. Ever since we've got Swantika and Dhwani, this house has changed. It's become a happy place. Man, that's the first thing Geetu said to me when we came home for the first time with the girls. She said, "Rajiv, the air, the very air of this house smells different. It *smells* happy!"' Rajiv looked at his happy place before continuing, 'Nikhil, I feel like I've been born again. Today, Nikhil, we are not celebrating those two new lives, I mean we aren't celebrating *just* those new lives. We are announcing also our own new lives, mine and Geetu's.'

And this, sober. Saying it sober was bad enough but *listening* to it sober? Juneja searched for an appropriate response. 'Happy Birthday, man! Seriously, Happy Birthday.'

Rajiv pulled him into a hug. 'Man, I *told* Geetu you'd understand. I *told* her Nikhil will be the *first* to wish me Happy Birthday.'

Juneja swallowed. It was hard to accept that he'd fulfilled Rajiv's expectations.

Thankfully, Rajiv's father interrupted. Geetu's

grandparents were retiring for the night and had to be driven to the guest house where they were putting up. Before Rajiv could make a move, Juneja offered to drive them over. He could just sneak off afterwards. Just then, Gagan came back with the orange juice.

'I'll come with you, sir. After all, they are *my* grandparents.'

And I'm taking them home, not adopting them. God, cut a man some slack.

The guest house was a stone's throw away and the deed done, Juneja sat in the car wondering how he could get rid of Gagan and sneak off.

'So Gagan, do you work hard, study hard, or play hard?'

'Sir, Nikhil, I've just finished B.Com. Pass and now Jiju, I mean Rajiv, is saying I could come to the city, I mean Delhi, and maybe start at the factory. He said I can do a management course in evening classes.'

I'll bet you did. Illiterate bastard.

'So, how about going somewhere for a beer?' Hell, it was worth a shot. When the dude said no, he'd at least have an excuse to leave.

Gagan went quiet.

Juneja was about to quit the scene when Gagan spoke up.

'Actually, sir, there is beer in the car.'

'In *this* car? In *my* car?'

'Yes, sir, Nikhil Sir, I mean, Jiju wanted me to buy some and I couldn't find the other car keys, so I took this and then there was no time to unload the car and—'

'It's OK, it's OK, you don't have to get so worked up. C'mon just chill.' *Hey, so what if the bugger took my car. He'd bought beer with it, hadn't he?*

Juneja pulled over in a shady by-lane near Rajiv's house. Inside, the music was raging unabated. Gagan went to the trunk and pulled out two beers.

Gagan was a cool guy, Juneja decided after a couple of beers. It was hardly his fault that he was from a small town, and now that he was moving to Delhi, he, Juneja, would show him how to have a good time. The working and studying hard he could manage on his own.

Juneja got out of the car to take a leak. Why piss on the road and get seen by Rajiv's lot? He went into a dark corner of Rajiv's garden and set about. God, beer really got the urethra going. Or was it the prostate it got going? He'd never quite understood if it was prostate or prostrate. It must surely be prostrate since it left you prostrate if it were meddled with. What then was prostate? Or was it actually pro-state and he'd been mispronouncing it all along like an asshole?

Juneja suddenly found a torch being aimed at him, resulting in a ray of light landing on his bum. He whirled around. An unfortunate act since it was accompanied by a fluid arc. He felt his genitals shrivel in shock. It was Geetu and her mother accompanied by the priest who'd conducted the morning pooja. They were coming to pick up the deities that had been deposited in a safe corner in the garden, away from the party. Deities he'd been caught pissing on.

At the same time, he realized that the music had been switched off and Gagan was retching in the background.

3 October 1999

White. Grey. The end of the world, the end of a friendship, the end of a relationship was white. It was the colour of the ceiling, seen from his bed, where he lay, not daring to move. Ever again. It was the colour of those wretched wailing women in front of the police station. They had painted his world white.

How could he colour his world again? Simple, just auto-delete the last twenty-four hours. Get rid of last night. Get it undone. At least get rid of the memories of last night.

Failing that, go to Arse.

All roads led to Arse.

At least it seemed that way. The road to Miraat was a little off the Jaipur highway and after following it for some time, the road signs started announcing the impending arrival of Pankot and Arse. Pankot, the other town with a police station, was just beyond Arse.

That Arse was sandwiched between Miraat and Pankot was a bit of a problem. Two states were both willing and unwilling to adopt it. This bizarre state of affairs had also been mentioned in the report. Two states shared jurisdiction in Arse and neither was too sure where the other's jurisdiction began or ended. But since there were two of them in the running, they naturally fought for complete control ... or total abdication. For example, nobody was very clear about what Arse's potential mineral wealth could be. It was unknown, i.e., no one was telling since neither state was willing to bear the cost of mining, nor was either state willing to bear the preliminary cost for the other state. During the elections, there were the usual tussles as to who was responsible for electricity, water and telephone. As a result, Arse had none.

That Arse had little to offer by way of tourist attractions was a further stick up its arse. Miraat had a fort and Pankot had some riverside bird sanctuary nonsense. But Arse itself offered only some strange temple ruins. These sites were supposedly witness to some atrocities during the revolt of 1857. Bloodbath of the English gentry. The report claimed that the locals were, in fact, not to blame for the bloodbath. Apparently, queerly inclined Englishmen had been misusing the holy temple for gay activities. The local populace had helplessly borne witness to this gross abuse of their beloved temple. But, in 1857, when the Raj had wobbled for a bit, the locals seized control (and other English body parts) with both hands.

A police station was to be found only in Miraat or in Pankot, both of which had formal individual state affiliations. As there was no local police in Arse, residents of Pankot and Miraat tended to dash down to this paradise for a quick spot of killing, assault, robbery, etc. This problem was solved by consigning the criminals to the jail of the town where they came from, i.e., Miraat criminals in the Miraat jail, Pankot criminals in Pankot's. This also enabled their respective families to visit them, noted the report. The average Arse citizen, the report suggested, was a peace- loving one who committed no crimes. Or perhaps since neither state wanted to sponsor the cost of Arse criminals, they were all being let off scot-free. In fact, this was another reason why a top cop had to be car dashed from Delhi: crimes were being committed in Arse, a road scam was being perpetrated there. Were the Arsians doing it? Or was it the usual Pankot and Miraat dwellers? And if it was indeed the Arsians, what should be done about them? The report mentioned that criminal Arsians could, in turn, also be car dashed to Delhi. However, now that Delhi was also a state and the cost of the penal system came from the state budget, Delhi wasn't too keen on Arsian perps either.

Similarly, the Public Distribution System (PDS) in Arse was also problematic. The central government had had to set up an exclusive system for Arse, whereby supplies were sent to each individual Arse household at reduced prices. This, explained the report, was because Pankot and Miraat residents had corrupted the original PDS set up in Arse by forging identity and ration cards. In fact, there had been riots in both towns over the decision to turn Arse over to the central government—a decision that was arrived at primarily because the two states involved had turned their backs on the village stuck as a pain in their bottom in the first place. Why, demanded Pankotias and Miraatis alike, should only Arse be favoured with better quality supplies from the Centre while they had to make do with state supplies of oil, rice and lentils, which were inedible?

Juneja pondered over the mysteries of crime as he sped along. The Miraat road was really very good. Which state was responsible?

It was just past nine in the morning and he was feeling a little hungry. After the disaster of the previous evening, he'd slunk home and run out at the speed of light at the crack of dawn. A quick shower, a brief call to Sanjana (answering machine) to tell her he was going and he was off.

Diwan Singh was probably still asleep after his toils of the day before; so there had been no breakfast except for a short tobacco meal washed down with instant coffee.

A smidgeon of victuals would alleviate the grumbling. He pulled over at a small cottage that advertised a full English breakfast as well as western-style lunch and tea and dinner. The house was surrounded by rose bushes. It bore the title: Moses' Toes. To illustrate the point further, a fat man was pointing at his toes, which were in fact blooming roses.

The interior was charmingly furnished. Old teak furniture and gleaming brass pots made an eye-catching contrast to the stone floor. Although this was clearly an eating area, an effort had been made to make it look more informal. The arrangement suggested a cosy easiness rather than rigid white table clothes and silver. Some of the tables were covered in gingham, others were bare, some offered books and one came equipped with a mahogany pipe rest. The air smelt of wood polish and roses with an underlying smoky flavour. The smoker must have left sometime ago—the room was quite empty.

'Sir?'

The apparition in white could only be described as a bearer.

'Breakfast?'

'Of course, sir. Full English breakfast, sir, or Indian?'

The English was spoken by an Indian, and the accent was Indian, but the disdain for Indian breakfast was distinctly foreign.

'What is English and what is Indian?'

The bearer gracefully indicated a corner table. It offered newspapers which by the look of them had been ironed.

'Sir, English breakfast is two pork sausages, toast, and a side order of two eggs, done to order and baked beans, mushrooms and a grilled tomato. With that, your beverage of choice, coffee or tea. Indian breakfast is an Indian bread of the day with vegetables and a hot beverage of your choice.'

Juneja swallowed. Where was this dude from?

'I'll have the English beverage of choice. Breakfast, I mean.'

'How would you like your eggs, sir?

After last night? Intact, I think. 'Scrambled.' *That's how they still feel.*

'Tea, or perhaps coffee?'

'Tea.'

'Indian, Chinese or Herbal?'

'Indian.' *And proud of it. Or not?*

'Very good, sir.'

It was a journey back in time. A journey back to the Raj. Not so surprising, perhaps. Pankot was an old favourite of the Raj that had lost favour as Simla had become more and more popular. Miraat was an old feudal state, still vaguely governed by a princely family. Some Anglo-Indian Eurasian Mrs Smith/Baker/Tailor-type of chick had probably been running this place for the past fifty years.

He picked up the thick leather-bound menu. The prices couldn't be much in a joint like this. On the first page was Moses with his floral feet, followed by a verse:

Moses supposes his toeses are roses,

But Moses supposes erroneously.

For nobody's toeses are poses of roses

As Moses supposes his toeses to be.

Interesting. Proceed to the prices. English breakfast. Rs 400. *Jesus Christ. How many poses does that buy?*

Juneja turned to the decidedly slim copies of the *Miraat Daily* and *Pankot Times* that had been placed for his perusal. The Hindi newspapers, which were obviously read by the local populace, were in a magazine rack in a corner. They were unironed and untouched.

Not surprisingly, both newspapers babbled about the road scam. Both were also distinctly Arse-neutral. The general tenor seemed to be that some bastard, mean type of people, who were antisocial and creepy and all things nasty, were bent on preventing—one newspaper used the word 'obstructing'—the course of development, not only in Arse but also in Pankot and Miraat. This was sacrilege and would not be borne silently by the courageous citizens of A, P & M. *Right. Still no clarification on whether Arsey or Arsian. Arsite?*

The teacup the bearer placed before him was fresh.

Fresh Darjeeling? Fresh Assam?

'What kind of tea is this?'

'Nilgiri, sir.'

Damnation.

'Who runs this place?'

'Sir, Moses' Toes is the property of my partner Moses and myself.'

His family was indeed Eurasian. No, not Anglo-Indian. *That's the reason Wonder Boy can prattle on in the Queen's English.*

'Your name?'

'Muk. Well, Mukesh really, but Muk to my friends.'

As if that explains anything.

Muk went to school in Delhi. After that he went to university in England. To university, mind you, not college. Since his Anglo aunty, the wife of his father's migrant brother who had no children, had been willing to sponsor him. His own family was ensconced in Delhi.

The years at Jesus College had made him realize that home was India, albeit with an English flavour. Must have made him realize quite a few other things as well, thought Juneja nastily. Jesus College. What kind of name was that? Most people Juneja knew had gone to Oxford or Cambridge. Obviously this idiot had only gotten admission to Jesus College.

Rose Cottage was the original name of the house. It had been the property of some Englishman who'd died trying to translate some Urdu poetry about wine and women. He'd taken the entire thing a bit too seriously and finally kicked the bucket, drowning in alcohol surrounded by six children from his three wives and one mistress. Muk had been able to buy the whole thing for a song. With his partner whom he'd met in Jesus College. The very same partner who was scrambling his eggs right now. Moses.

Also, neither Moses nor Muk had surnames. They didn't seem to believe in them.

Juneja got this entire verbal diarrhoea more or less immediately after he'd confessed to being the Delhi policeman in charge of the road scam.

The breakfast came borne by a small, brown-haired, chef-type person with startlingly green eyes.

'Moses?'

'Hi,' the voice was deep and cultured, 'I'm Muk's partner, Moses. I just overheard, you're the policeman down from Delhi?'

'I am.'

'Do begin with the food. We can talk later over coffee.'

'Tea,' corrected Muk.

The breakfast was excellent. The eggs scrambled to perfection, the sausages softly pink on the inside, and the tomatoes slightly charred and tangy. Whether it was worth the 400 bucks was another story.

He polished off the entire rack of toast and was wondering whether he'd be able to eat more when Moses ended the mystery by appearing with an enormous pot of tea. An old-fashioned teapot. It was probably an antique Denby. It was accompanied by three cups and a small pitcher of milk, covered with a beaded lace doily.

So, there was going to be company for tea.

'Mind if I smoke?'

'Not if I can join you,' answered Moses. But he shook his head to the proffered cigarettes and took out a pipe instead.

At Juneja's unspoken surprise, he answered, 'Muk thinks it's healthier.'

Right. And that's obviously the important thing.

Muk appeared through the main door. He'd been collecting the mail. He shook his head in answer to Moses' questioning look, 'Nothing that can't wait. So, Mr Juneja ...'

'Call me Nikhil, please.'

Muk nodded graciously. 'The road scam?'

'Well, I'm here just to make inquiries, you know.'

'And where will you be putting up?'

Was that it? Was the entire thing just a ploy to make him stay here? Hell, he could do a lot worse.

'What would you suggest?'

Muk gave him a warm, approving smile. 'Well, here of course, but we are in Miraat, well really Arse–Miraat border.'

'I'm expected at the Miraat police station at midday and I need to see the arrangements that have been made for my stay. But I think, one way or the other, I'll be back for more beverages of my choice!'

After some more genial chit-chat, Juneja sped on. Moses, Poses, or whatever, seemed like a good idea. He decided he'd try and reject any accommodation arranged by the police. It would in any case be some shitty government rest house sort of place. All told, he was feeling a lot better after breakfast. Moses and Muk had had a sort of calming effect on him. The landscape was beautiful. Perhaps it was because Arse's mineral riches hadn't been exploited that the countryside was so unspoilt. No majestic mountains clamouring for your attention, or stark, stony desert-like landscape ruled by the Jakes and the Jareds of this world designed to make women swoon. The way to Arse was a soft, undulating green. Fields and fields of green stuff as far as the eye could see. There was little vehicular traffic. An odd car or two. Mostly two-wheelers or bicycles. Everything seemed soft, hushed, waiting. Juneja felt like he was going back in time, to a past where things were simple. Relationships, friends, work—the entire business of life in Delhi—appeared to be slipping away. Not that he was trying to hang on to them. The verdant countryside seemed to plead with him to forget the city.

Like Muk had said, just where Arse began, there was a small rickety path on the left. This was a short cut to the police station which had been strategically placed at the very edge of Arse and Miraat. Moses had said that Pankot's police station was similarly placed, a fact that the report had confirmed. Such a placement of the two police stations afforded swift and speedy response to and resolution of crimes, assured the report.

The Miraat police station bore an uncanny resemblance to Moses Poses, as Juneja had decided to call it. It sure as hell looked like no other police station he had ever seen. It wasn't an ancient cottage, but it was, well, for lack of a better word, cute. It was small and cosy, and surrounded by tender green fields.

Outside, two policemen sat playing cards. One was a youngish chap, in his late twenties, lanky, fair. The other was considerably older. Juneja's age, give or take five years.

They didn't jump to their feet at the sight of Juneja. How should they know who he was? But they must have felt that the flashy, red car demanded some sort of acknowledgement.

'Good morning, sir!'

'Morning! I'm looking for S.P. Joshi.'

The other policeman rose and extended a courteous hand. 'Joshi!'

'Hello! Additional Commissioner Nikhil Juneja, from Delhi.'

'We were expecting you on Monday, sir.'

The other one butted in, 'Hope you had a good drive, sir. Not too many traffic jams.'

On a Sunday? Dimwit.

Juneja ignored the first and sidestepped the second. Since when did he owe these or any other punks an explanation?

Rajiv and the happenings of last night were best forgotten. Least said, soonest mended.

'I'm afraid I had to stop for directions. I wasn't expecting a police station in such a beautiful setting.'

'My colleague … or rather, *our* colleague, Inspector Gupte. Let us go inside and discuss the details. I am having my papers and a copy of the report that was sent to Delhi. I'm sure the discussion will be progressing better with a cup of tea. Or would you be preferring coffee?'

'Tea is fine,' answered Juneja. *Darjeeling rather than Assam.*

'Gupte, two Tetleys. After you, sir.'

They settled down in a room that looked decidedly underused. No masses of files lined the corridor. The table bore an empty *in* tray. The *out* tray contained perhaps a dozen-odd sheets of paper.

Juneja fiddled with his cigarette packet a little, so that Joshi had time to unearth an ashtray. It also gave Gupte time to appear with vile-tasting, orange-coloured tea.

'So, Joshi, what can you tell me about the road scam? As you know, the Centre is quite worried.'

'Sir, I can't explain it. You see, because of Arse's unique position, the situation is very strange. We have never been having this kind of thing before. Now, Miraat and Pankot have clear identities. They know where they are belonging. But Arse has not been having a clear state affiliation and so they are developing their own systems. They are not even coming under Panchayati Raj because we are not knowing which Block Samiti to allot them to! Therefore in Arse they are having a unique administrative set-up of their own. Almost as if they were a, a …' Joshi paused to pull the tea tray towards himself. He added three teaspoons of the unrefined sugar to each cup in an absent-minded sort of way.

Juneja swallowed. This was going to be fun. The first sip reminded him of strong, sweet urine. He lit up again, trying to focus on how to get rid of the tea.

'You were saying, Joshi?'

'Yes, sir, sorry, I mean they are having their own life, in which we don't interfere. We have never needed to. And their life is very happy because their products are the cheapest here, so everyone is buying things from Arse. Like this sugar, sir. We are calling it sweet brown sugar.' Joshi gave an accompanying little laugh, which Juneja completely ignored.

He asked without sparing the stinking goo another glance, 'What d'you mean, this sugar?'

'Sir, it is from Arse. Surely it isn't white sugar, like you will get in Delhi or in all big shops in Miraat or Pankot. But it is costing only Rs 1.75 per kilo.'

'So?' asked Juneja. Who bought strange brown stuff in the name of sugar?

'Sir, all the budget-conscious people nearby are going to Arse. Arse is getting special concessions from the Centre and therefore it is being able to produce things at these prices. So rural unemployment or any kind of financial difficulty is not a problem here. The people are being very contented and happy. That is why we are also not having any case of criminality or anything.'

'None?' asked doubting Juneja.

'Sir, sometimes some boy or youth will be getting drunk, some pilferage and such things may be happening. After all people are people. But no robbery, murder, assault ... nothing serious. Very peace-loving people. Sir, also another thing is that Arse's products are very healthy. This sugar is not tasting like white sugar but it is healthy because it is being made naturally.'

Juneja tried not to look disbelieving. Western ideas had evidently percolated down to Arse. If it stank, tasted and looked like shit, was it shit? No! It was organic. The fact that this shit was organic did not make it better, if you asked Juneja, who would have strongly preferred carcinogenic sugar.

'So the stuff is organic?'

'No, sir, not at all. It is purely vegetarian.'

Top that, Nikhil.

'No, I mean handmade,' tried Juneja for lack of a better word. Besides, wasn't crappy handmade stuff like pottery and all organic?

'Yes, sir, in fact most products are having to be handmade because that is one thing where Arse is having a problem. They are having electricity only for two hours in the morning from Pankot and two hours in the evening from Miraat. Both towns are not being able to spare more. During the day, when they are making sugar and all, no electricity is being made available to them. Also water supply is available only at these times.'

'And they don't mind having no electricity? That means no TV!'

'Sir, they are very closed people. They are not liking influences from outside. Everyone is knowing this.'

'Are you from Arse?'

'No, sir, from Miraat itself. That is why I can say. Other people, when they come to Arse, maybe they are being surprised but we people from Miraat, from Pankot, we know. We know that they are not wanting to have TV or anything like this.'

'I notice you call it Urse, I was told it's Ur-sé.'

'Sir, it is said, when the English were here, they were trying to teach the people English. But they were not being able to pronounce the word *earth*. They were calling it *Urse*, so the name stuck.'

Hmm. Urse. 'Ursed if I understand that.

'So what was the original name?'

'Sir, what origin, it was just a subdistrict. No name.'

Juneja pulled out his report. 'You wrote this?'

'Yes, sir, I mean Gupte and myself.'

Juneja automatically translated this into laurels for Joshi and the transference of all possible errors to Gupte.

OK. Enough waffling. Time to get down to the important stuff. 'What arrangements have been made for my stay?'

Joshi was obviously prepared. He reached for a list in the *out* tray. A contribution of the efficient Gupte?

'Sir, there is Hotel Vikram in Pankot, three stars, Rose Cottage Moses' Toes, no stars, and Home Stay in Pankot.'

Interesting way of putting it. Moses Poses had more stars than the rest of them put together, but since it wasn't a registered hotel, one could pass it off as no stars.

Juneja played for time.

'What is this Home Stay?'

'Sir, like small hotel only. Gupte's family is running it.'

Right. And you have a connect with Hotel Vikram.

Could either have a connection with Moses?

Unlikely. They wouldn't have said it's 'no stars' otherwise.

'So Gupte is from Pankot?'

'Yes, sir, in both stations, Pankot and Miraat, we are having mixed police force because of Arse.'

'And this Home Stay and Vikram place, they have TV?'

Outwitted and overtrumped, Joshi shook his head sadly.

'No, sir, but both places are having telephone service.'

'I don't need telephone service. I have my mobile.'

'Sir, mobile is not working here, sir, because of Arse's—'

'Unique position,' finished Juneja. *Hmm*. 'So who should I speak to in Arse regarding the situation?'

'Sir, I myself have made an appointment with Mr Raghavendra Pratap Singh for you. He is belonging to the most important family here in the Miraat–Pankot region.'

Raghavendra Pratap Singh, ascertained Joshi, was in the fields, talking to some farmers. A few telephone calls ensured he would wait there for them. It was round the corner, said Joshi, they could go on foot. Juneja's heart sank. Meet some old fogey in a field? That was the end of his trousers and his leather shoes. *Bloody village boors.* Screw up his clothes and then expect him to suck some bloody sugarcane for lunch, no doubt …

They went over to the adjacent fields where a group of men could be seen. A charpoy had been laid out and a young man sat on it, drinking from a steaming cup.

As they made their way to it, he got up.

'Hi, I'm Raghu!'

Juneja stuck his hand into the tanned, muscular one being proffered, feeling somewhat bemused. This was not what he had expected. Raghavendra Pratap Singh had sounded like a seventy-year-old patriarch gurgling into his hookah. It had turned out to be a good-looking forty-something. Raghavendra Pratap Singh was tanned, rather slim, and decidedly handsome. The moustache was clipped and not the Hulk Hogan or WWF-type muttonchops he'd expected. The English was public school and the clothes designer. The air, of course, was royal.

'What can I offer you, Mr Jun—'

'Nikhil, Nikhil, please.'

Raghu gave him a winning smile. 'I'll bet a cup of tea will do you good. Did Joshi give you—' He broke off and started laughing at Juneja's expression. 'So you *did* get the royal welcome! Tea with a spoonful of Arse's best!'

'A spoonful? More like a tablespoonful!' said Juneja ruefully, not quite daring to look at the wooden-faced Joshi standing next to him.

Raghu seemed to have no qualms about giving offence. 'More tea? Guaranteed, without sugar?'

Juneja tried to think of a politic way of getting his hands on some alcohol. Demand that his health required him to guzzle 40 proof? When he got back to Delhi, he'd talk to a doctor and find out the name of some such malady. If nothing else, it would at least prevent him from drinking urinal tea.

As if reading his thoughts, Raghu broke in, 'You know, it's time for lunch. Or an early lunch in any case. Why don't we, ummm, crack a few beers and talk, followed by lunch?'

A man after his own heart.

'Why don't we do just that?'

'Joshi, you take our guest home in your car,' and turning to Juneja, he indicated the gleaming BMW parked on the other side of the field. 'Sorry, I'm on my mobike; wasn't expecting company in the fields!'

'What should I do with my car?'

'Oh! I didn't realize you had a vehicle. Let Joshi drive. I'd have suggested you drive yourself, but the roads here are rather poor and take some time getting used to. I suggest you give yourself a few days getting used to them before you risk your machine.'

Juneja gave a slow nod. The air was distinctly royal.

Joshi drove him through Arse to Raghu's ancestral property in Pankot. The village was like a small jewel, glittering in the setting of lush green fields. The acrid dust and heat of Delhi were like a distant nightmare. It was hard to believe that this paradise could be reached in a matter of hours. It seemed to exist not just in another country but in a different lifetime, in a different time zone.

The streets were cobbled, if at all. Everywhere, people were busy working. Women grinding flour by hand. Baking bread at the community oven. Men working in fields, with a plough and oxen. Basket weaving, embroidery ... and all the products the region was famous for being made by hand. It was the ease and seriousness with which they worked that amazed Juneja. He heard no raised voices. No friendly evocations to go fuck one's own self/sister/mother. The pace was unhurried, almost relaxed. Yet the people didn't give the impression of dawdling.

But the real difference was in the air. Juneja was amazed at the difference the lack of electricity made. The lack of machines, Joshi pointed out, meant a lack of pollution. But to Juneja, the air was not only cleaner, it appeared lighter, clearer.

Juneja had thought this was only his pathetic big-city outlook, till Joshi clarified, 'Sir, you will think air here is lighter. Because here we are not receiving radio and they are not having electricity, so no TV, sir, so everything is quieter. Air is light.'

Juneja nodded slowly. It was true. This was a blessed country. The people were shy but obviously welcoming. He had been the recipient of numerous delighted smiles. The people were busy and happy. It was like a dream.

'So does Arse have a lot of tourists?'

'Not really, sir. You see, today people are not wanting rooms without TV and all. In the sixties, for a short time, there was a hotel here. All those hippies and all came here for free life. But that did not last very long because people here were not being favourable.'

'So where is this hotel now?'

'Sir, it is being used as storage area for sugar and grain.'

'Who does it belong to?'

'Sir, Mr Raghavendra Pratap Singh's father built it. First as a school and then, when the school did not succeed, as a hotel.'

'What do you mean "school did not succeed"?'

'Sir, there is no school in Arse. A few families are sending their children to government school in Pankot or Miraat, but since their traditional means of livelihood is farming, many families are thinking it is a waste of time to be sending the children to school because it is taking up too much time. The children are not having any good means of transportation because of lack of road and therefore are going with traditional means of transportation—bullock cart. It is taking a very long time. Also, sir, sometimes weather conditions are not permitting said method of transportation for children.'

Ask not what you can do for bureaucracy, reflected Juneja, finding himself quite prostrate at Joshi's turn of phrase. Ponder instead on what bureaucracy can do for your linguistic abilities.

Joshi had been quite conscious of driving Juneja's fancy car. But Juneja noticed true reverence in his manner when they pulled up before a high gate. It was the family mansion. The BMW pulled up and quivered like a silver bullet.

'OK, Joshi, Juneja Sir will contact you when he needs to.'

The mansion, like everything else he'd seen so far, was from another age. It was huge and impeccably maintained. An army of minions scurried about seeing to the endless demands the upkeep of such a palace necessarily entailed. It was a tranquil beehive of buzzing busyness. Nonetheless, each and every person made it a point to stop whatever they were doing and pay obeisance to Raghu, who in turn acknowledged the greeting gravely, much to Juneja's surprise.

'I've been telling them to stop, you know, but old habits die hard. I tell them the Raj is over but they say that I, or rather, we, the family, will always be their ruler. Quite embarrassing, really.'

Juneja would normally have scoffed at the self-effacement but, combined with the returned greeting, he was quite perplexed. Perhaps when you were ultra rich, the effacement was yet another thing you could afford.

The terrace was as huge as was suitable for such a large mansion. Potted plants and cane furniture completed the casual, country look.

Raghu indicated a chair with an airy gesture and pulled out a cigarette from a case. Battered but silver. The genuine thing.

He spoke, answering Juneja's unasked questions. 'You know, this house has been in my family for at least the past three hundred years. My family, my wife and my children live in Calcutta most of the time. My parents migrated there years ago. Today they'd like to come back here but the lack of proper medical care in this part makes that impossible. If this road came up in the next few years, it would make possible my parents' dream of returning and also improve the lives of all those who live here.'

Juneja took time pulling out his own cigarettes. Nothing had prepared him for the speed at which things had moved. He'd expected to be squatting with some village yokels, narrowing down on the local criminals who could be rounded up to make enquiries. Instead, he was lounging amongst the super rich who wanted his help. It would imply, screamed Juneja's well-honed instincts, that there was big money at stake here.

He lit up slowly, enjoying the smell of spices that was slowly drifting out of some hidden corner, mingling with the smell of freshly watered earth and of the colourful flowers in the vase on their table.

A little small talk to begin with, perhaps. 'I notice you call it Arsh. Is that how it's pronounced?'

'My father says it's a bastardization of the word "Sparsh" meaning touch. The word was synonymous with the region because of all the handicrafts that were made here.'

Right. Great. Really interesting. 'So who do you think is responsible for the pilferage of the materials, Raghu? Any ideas?'

Raghu too, it appeared, was fumbling for words. Perhaps he'd expected a policeman of Sinha's calibre and was equally nonplussed.

Raghu looked at the still smouldering cigarette in his hand and looked about for a minion who'd bring an ashtray. Seemingly out of nowhere, Juneja saw a servant holding an ashtray appear behind Raghu's shoulder. Juneja was about to reach over to use it when a hesitant movement behind his own shoulder caught his eye. Another human ashtray stood waiting for an ashen deposit.

Raghu smiled and shook his head. He turned and gently removed the ashtray from the servant's hand and said in Hindi, 'You have a guest. Won't you offer him a glass of water even?'

Before the abashed man could answer, a young girl approached the table with a tray. She placed chilled glasses of what appeared to be lassi in front of them, as well as a bottle of water and two extra glasses.

Raghu laughed and turned to the silent man behind him. 'I knew you would never let us down! We'll have a couple of beers before lunch. We'll eat in the small lunchroom.'

He turned to Juneja who had allowed himself the liberty of pouring out a glass of water. 'This feudal thing is terrible. You know this kind of behaviour is impossible to buy. My wife always says that we should take people from here over to Calcutta. The help there is impossible.'

'So why don't you?'

Raghu looked rueful. 'I tried. My wife had unfortunately expressed the very same sentiment in front of the people here. After that there was no stopping them. Nothing would stop them from coming with us.'

He looked down for a few seconds and poured himself a glass of water.

'Nikhil, it was a disaster. They are a very gentle people. They were pushed around, cheated, looted. At the end of two months, one was sick, one was chronically homesick and depressed and the third committed suicide. Not because he was unhappy. God, Nikhil, that was the worst of it. He left behind a letter, saying, he couldn't bear to live because he'd failed us.'

Juneja felt his otherwise healthy sense of derision leave him. It was a strange feeling.

'I had the other two return as soon as possible. My wife was inconsolable and blamed herself. My mother went into a depression. God, it was terrible!'

Episode 2: Further Confessions of a Reluctant King was temporarily interrupted by the arrival of the same young girl. She knelt down next to the table and, from the tray, placed two bottles of beer, an opener and two frosted glasses on the table.

Juneja had to strain his ears to hear her soft murmur. 'Shall I remove the other glasses?'

Raghu nodded his assent before commanding Juneja, 'Leave the lassi, man, it'll just fill up your stomach! Have beer instead!'

Juneja smiled his agreement and the girl started removing the untouched glasses.

Raghu reached out and gently brushed her cheek with his knuckles. She swallowed but made no effort to move away. It was an affectionate gesture, like a father with a shy child.

After she had left, Raghu said, 'You know Nikhil, you must be wondering why I'm telling you so much so fast. I know, it's a lot of unorganized information. Tomorrow we can talk in more detail after you've had time to process all that I've thrown at you. But I just wanted you to know as soon as possible how disturbed I, no, not just *I* am, but how disturbed *we all* are. This road will make a huge difference to all our lives. Look at this girl who was just here. Kasturi. Her life in Arse will change. She doesn't have to be a maidservant. Maybe a college can be made here. No, there is no *maybe*, my family will ensure that a college is made here. But we can't make it if there are no teachers willing to come here. My father tried with a school—'

'I know, Joshi showed it to me. He said it's now used as a store.'

'A store! A bloody store! It's a joke, Nikhil, a bloody poor one at that.' Raghu shook his head. 'And you know what, Nikhil, the damn school is really a bloody lousy store. The furniture was made of wood and got eaten up by termites in the first two years of disuse. We had to get the entire place fumigated so it could be used as a store. What a bloody joke!'

The small lunchroom was appropriately magnificent and the food and drink lavish, but Juneja was careful to imbibe prudently. The Big Discussion would happen after the meal, he was sure. Lunch was restricted to social chit-chat and the usual platitudes peculiar to upper-class Delhi. Public schools were identified and compared, they moved on to clubs in Delhi versus clubs in Calcutta, leading to whether the confectionery of Old Delhi was the real thing ... it was an endless list of trivia. One day, thought Juneja, in order to keep up with the times, he'd have to pick up the finer points of wine. So far he'd learnt that they were dry and sweet as opposed to the lot of them being wet. He was also planning to cultivate cigar smoking to impress Sanjana, but hadn't got very far till now. He'd read that the things had to be kept in a humidor, which was a kind of lobster, wasn't it? Diwan Singh, given his current religious fervour, would never put up with animal carcasses containing tobacco products.

After lunch, a choice of tea or coffee was offered. Browned off by Nilgiri and Tetley, Juneja opted for coffee. It would hopefully help fight off postprandial somnolence. He half expected the volley of Columbian, Brazilian, decaf or Turkish and was quite happy when he got Nescafe cooked to a twist. It *would* wake him up.

'So, Raghu, you need to tell me about the situation here. What's your take on it?' *Off with the gloves!*

'I don't really know about my take on it, Nikhil, but I'll be happy to tell you what I do know about the situation, as you're calling it.'

Touché.

'It all started about three months back. As you know

there are no main roads in Arse. The plan was to set up a main arterial road connecting Arse with Pankot and Miraat. With time, further roads would be built, depending on how the situation develops. Since there has never been a road here, it is currently impossible to ascertain what the impact of such a road would be. According to the report we commissioned, what Arse requires most is a school and a hospital. But the road will obviously make a huge impact on the economic situation in Arse. The entire economic mobility of the village as such is—'

'Yes, Raghu, but from the report I have, the village is against the road project because compensation is more or less on the basis of caste.'

Raghu got up to call for more coffee. They were sitting in a lounge of sorts. Well, if you call a long, high-ceilinged room full of portraits of strange moustachioed ancestors and heads of animals they'd hunted a lounge.

'No, I'd rather just have some water,' said Juneja as the servant came in with a tray bearing a thermos of hot coffee and a carafe of water. *A thermos! How classy!*

'Nikhil,' said Raghu quietly after the servant had closed the door, 'this caste business is quite frankly just an interpretation of things. Whether or not this is the case will come out only once we know who the culprit is.'

'Whose interpretation?'

Raghu heaved a sigh and smiled ruefully. 'Mine, Joshi's, Gupte's. What should I say? That anyone from Arse can be opposed to the road project is unthinkable.'

'So it's the good old foreign hand?'

'Well, it's an outside hand, for sure.'

'Raghu, please. Even if Arse doesn't have a clear Indian state affiliation, it can't be the *Pakistanis* who are to blame!'

Raghu smiled at Juneja's cynicism. The Pakistanis! Failing all else, they could always be counted on to provide a suitable scapegoat. But Arse was India's very own problem and unfortunately, inconveniently away from the border.

Juneja leaned forward. 'Let me put my cards on the table, Raghu. The Centre is worried. You, Joshi ... *someone*, has sent a report to Delhi. In this report, it is claimed that the building material sent to Arse for the purpose of developing a road has been pilfered and tampered with on a scale that is hindering this road project.' Juneja paused to swallow some coffee and light a cigarette. Had he really been on the verge of saying 'aforementioned road project'? He might as well start speaking vide a letter dated the last century soon.

'Furthermore, it is claimed in the report that this tampering and pilferage is happening because of problems regarding compensation which, the people of Arse say, is along the lines of caste. Now you're telling me this is a load of bollocks.' *Aforementioned report is now mentioned bollocks.*

It was the Moment of Truth. Juneja assumed a pose of suggestive menace, waiting to pounce on the denouement ahead.

It didn't come.

'Nikhil, this is the reason I wanted you to come here.

Or rather someone like you. Someone who'd understand, not some dickhead like Joshi.'

Oh, I bollock you and you dickhead me?

'There are no caste issues. The problem is just the pilferage. Most of the land required for the road belongs to the family. There are a few other farmers who are nominally affected, but we're talking about just a handful of people here. And they have certainly said nothing to me or anyone else about caste-based compensation.'

'They are satisfied with the compensation they have been offered?'

'Yes, of course they are. In fact, they were more than satisfied with the offer we made them.'

'*You* offered them compensation?'

'Well, it makes more sense for the road developer to buy from a single landowner rather than to negotiate with fragmented small farmers. So we decided that we would buy the land necessary for the road and a single sale would be made to the developer.'

'So why the entire rigmarole about caste?' asked Juneja, bemused.

'Nikhil, I'm going to be very open with you. We had to have a big issue to get a senior policeman to come down here. The Centre would never send a policeman for something as petty as pilferage.'

Hmm, cast your eyes on a big fish, did you?

Juneja suddenly felt enormously tired. The rigours of the past twenty-four hours were more than he could bear any more.

'Raghu, I'm sorry, but we're going to have to postpone this conversation. I fear I have a severe migraine coming on.'

It was a bit abrupt, but Juneja had learnt that migraines were a sudden, severe and as such, golden ailment.

'Of course, Nikhil, of course. Look, let's meet up tomorrow at, say, eleven? My man will drop you off now. No, no,' he overruled as Juneja tried to protest, 'you're tired and you've got a migraine. Those are hardly appropriate circumstances to race the Arse 500!'

Moses Poses was really the right choice. Muk and Moses waived away the entire check-in procedure, saying it could wait till the morn. The room he was shown by a smiling but thankfully quiet Muk was spacious and well appointed. The furniture was worn out but tasteful and somehow seemed eminently suitable.

He decided against dinner, telling Muk he was going to turn in early. But first of all, he needed to touch base. Juneja tried his cell phone but there was no reception, as Joshi had promised.

The shower provided some welcome relief to his injured spirit and he felt the stress of the day gradually ease off. Perhaps it wasn't such a bad idea being away from Delhi for a few days. His father could sing for an answer to his stupid offer and Rajiv, well he didn't want to think about bloody Rajiv *or* his stupid children *or* brother-in-law or anyone.

As for Sanjana, well Sanjana should learn, in any case, that he couldn't always be at her beck and call. He'd left written instructions for Diwan Singh, telling him to inform

Sanjana where he was. Although Diwan Singh didn't overly approve of her, he was reliable. Sanjana would then obviously try his cell phone and finding it out of limits would scream blue murder, but that was perhaps also not such a bad idea. She needed to know who the boss was.

The warm shower left him feeling seriously relaxed and he changed into a loose T-shirt and shorts for the night. He pulled out the bottle of Laphroaig, intending to settle down to a well-earned drink.

Just then, there was a knock on the door.

'Yes?'

'Hi, Nikhil!' It was Moses this time. 'Sorry, I don't want to disturb you but I couldn't help hearing the water running. So I guessed you were still awake. A call came through for you from Delhi.' He proffered a piece of paper.

'Thanks for taking the message. It's no problem. I wasn't intending to turn in for the night yet.' Juneja looked at the paper. Gupta. *Hmm, must have got the number from Gupte or Joshi.* Then, without being quite sure why he was doing it, he said, 'Join me for a drink?'

Moses looked startled, but a quick glance at the label made his craggy face crease into a smile. 'The Scottish God's gift to mankind? Sure! Hang on a second and I'll tell Muk where I am, and get us some decent glasses.'

Share his Laphroaig with the local riff-raff? The friendly neighbourhood gay? What had he been thinking of? *That's the problem with you, Nikhil, a smarmy accent and white skin and you're inviting all and sundry to your room.*

The fucker had now run off to get his silly, wimpy boyfriend who'd also slug away at Juneja's bottle. Free booze—nothing attracted the flies faster.

Juneja also decided to take the opportunity to change his shorts for a pair of trousers. No point letting a fairy ogle the family jewels. That too for free.

Moses returned in ten minutes with some fancy crystal glasses and small bowls of munchies balanced on a tray.

Juneja forced himself to ask, 'Muk's not joining us?'

'Nah, he's a teetotaller. So it's really great to have company. Also, I must confess, good liquor is something I really miss in India.'

Juneja smiled graciously. 'Good whisky needs good company.'

They settled down with the drinks and an awkward silence that Juneja broke. 'So what brought you to India, Moses? Besides the bad liquor?'

Moses smiled. 'Well, Muk, I suppose.'

'Right.' *Well done, Nikhil, really convincing. Try again.*

'Well, your Raghu Pratap Singh certainly gave me reason to stay today!'

'Ah, my feudal lord!'

'Is he?'

'Well a benevolent dictator, certainly. Goes with the turf, doesn't it?'

'How d'you mean?'

'Nikhil, the family … actually, around here, there is only *one* family. The Family. When people say "the house" it's their House, "the family" it's their Family. It's the way it is. When two towns and a village think you're a direct descendant from up above, you'd have to be Gandhi not to believe at least some of it.'

Moses broke off and leaned forward to help himself to some peanuts. But he didn't eat them immediately.

'Something the matter?'

'No, not at all, Nikhil, just thinking. I … we both, Muk and I, get along really well with Raghu. His father is strictly old school but Raghu's a nice bloke. Uncomplicated, easy. He comes over every now and then. And I'm happy to have a beery evening. I haven't met his wife, but Muk tells me I'm not likely to.' He smiled ruefully. 'Some things *are* done differently here.'

Juneja smiled back. The thought of a young maharani entering a pub for a drink … *hmm*.

'But I still haven't got used to the way things are done here. It's all very, I really don't know. The Family decides everything. Sometimes I think we're quite lucky that Raghu gets along so well with us. His father certainly wasn't too thrilled to have the two of us queering up the local pitch.'

Juneja tried to pretend he didn't understand that and hoped the twinkle in Moses' eye was a reflection of the light.

But Moses let it pass. 'But when I think Raghu could have been against us too … well, I don't know. I really don't know,' he trailed off, rather lamely, to Juneja's mind.

'So why the entire road scam? If you're saying that the entire area is so totally under his control, then who would do something like this? And that too on a scale that jeopardizes the entire project?'

'That's just it, Nikhil, I don't know.'

'OK, even if some asshole is against this project, why doesn't Raghu put the project on hold, find the asshole and beat the crap out of him in the good old feudal style? And don't tell me things aren't usually done like that, Moses!'

'Between you, me and this divine Scotch, Nikhil, I think Raghu has political ambitions. So beating the crap out of the local populace is probably not a very good idea right now. He needs a successful project to get a party ticket. But that is just my suspicion. I do, however, know that Raghu has too much money riding on this project to be able to afford any more delays.'

'Huh? Raghu has money invested in the project?'

'Raghu *is* the project. His company, R.P. Singh Transports, is developing the road.'

Juneja fell asleep in a mildly intoxicated, highly euphoric state. The conversation had yielded a fair amount of food for thought.

They'd polished off more or less two-thirds of a litre bottle and, Juneja was happy to note, it was Moses who drank more—it allayed Juneja's secret fear of being an alcoholic, which he most certainly was not. At Sanjana's bidding he'd been doing strange ten-point tests on the Internet—the 'if your answer to any of these questions is yes, you have an alcohol problem' variety. He'd had a few yeses but had confessed none to Sanjana.

Moses had been happy to drink, claiming it did him good since he so rarely had the opportunity to do so. He told Juneja about all the problems he and Muk had had to face. Moses had lost his parents at an early age and had put himself through school and university in the UK on the smallish sum of money that he'd inherited and subsequently spent. Then he'd met Muk. And life, life itself had changed.

Juneja deigned to ask if it was The Life or merely normal people's life.

They returned to Delhi, looking forward to yet another life together. But Muk's family didn't approve of their relationship, which wasn't surprising. Most Indians were violently opposed to homosexuality and considered it a vile Western import. As far as he knew, Section 377 of the Indian Penal Code prohibited 'carnal intercourse against the order of nature'. It had often been used by Sajjan Kumar when he'd been on a park beat at night. He usually let off the fuckers for a fuck or a buck, depending on the beauty of the case.

But Muk's parents hadn't been willing to do anything of the sort. Instead, they'd accused Moses of polluting their son with his decadent Western ideas. Muk's mother had also called Moses a *kothi*, which stunned Juneja, who didn't think anyone's mother could know such a word.

The ultimate straw was when Muk's sister implored them to leave for fear that no one would marry her. So they had left and finally settled down in this back of beyond place, where nobody knew them and they knew nobody. It was all rather traumatic for Moses, who had been harbouring dreams of learning authentic Indian cooking from his prospective mother-in-law, who'd instead told him to bugger off. Or failing that, to at least stop buggering her son.

Juneja hurriedly broke in to change the subject and told him that even without Mommy's help, he was a great cook. A real chef.

Moses smiled sadly. It was his passion. Albeit an amateur passion. He'd wanted to be a ballet dancer but he'd had too many injuries too early to make a professional career out of it.

Appalled that each and every preconceived stereotype he'd ever had about homosexual men was true, Juneja told him that he'd always admired the ballet.

Moses needed no further urging. Before Juneja could even applaud his enthusiasm, he launched into a series of horrendously fluid dance movements. It was as if there was some awful liquid, limpid music playing that only Moses could hear. To this music, he swayed and sashayed in a way that made Juneja want to kick his ass viciously, preferably from a window ... in a high building.

He would probably have plodded on in this vein, much to Juneja's increasing anguish, had Muk not appeared. The sight of his partner in pajamas and a dressing gown made Moses grind to a halt, but not without some more fluid head nods to the thankfully silent music.

They left despite Juneja's polite request to have another for the road. Or goad, he added silently, in his head. But they left. Or rather, Muk refused for both of them, citing the late hour, much to Juneja's relief.

Abandoning the trousers for his well-worn shorts, Juneja reflected on all he'd learnt. Gay men were dancers or cooks. Good cooks, terrible dancers. Mothers knew bad words, the kind that Sajjan Kumar wouldn't use in front of Juneja, and Raghu was planning to make a heap from the road project. What small bundle would he then place before Juneja? It was a happy thought. Juneja climbed into bed, looking forward to the next sunny day in Arse.

4 October 1999

Not surprisingly, Moses didn't put in an appearance during breakfast, Muk was tight-lipped and taciturn, and Juneja was anxious to be on his way.

Outside, the sun shone, birds chirped—in the trees and in his heart. Life is good, reflected Juneja, as he smartly avoided a pothole only to curse as he hit another.

It wasn't so much as a road as little stretches of level land that connected the potholes. The level stretches indicated that a pothole had come to an end. Otherwise the unwary traveller might just have thought that the road consisted of a hole. Was that mathematically possible, thought Juneja. If a hole was huge and did not end, would it not, perforce actually ... well at least in the middle part, be level? If that was the case, was it actually the level pieces of land that were making the potholed road appear potholed? Of course, the fact that it wasn't a tarred road and in fact just a rubble path that hadn't been cultivated was naturally an exacerbating factor.

The route, Muk had assured him, was a simple one. There was only one path in all of Arse. It led at one end to Miraat and at the other to Pankot. So all he had to do was to follow this single path and he would eventually find himself in the place he wanted to be. Or break an axle, whichever came first.

It was a strange feeling, driving on a road completely devoid of other vehicles. In fact there were hardly any people to be seen. He could see a few outlines on the horizon, working in the fields, but that was more or less all. A certain cussedness made him pull over and get out of the car. Were there really no people or were they hiding?

Outside was, if anything, even more disconcerting. A silence untouched by human voice choked all sound. He cleared his throat and pulled out a cigarette. The click of the lighter made him hear the birds twittering more clearly. It was a reassuring sound. Juneja felt like the lone survivor of a nuclear holocaust.

Must have been a good kind of holocaust—the sun is shining and warm, the birds are singing and I have a Lancer that's survived!

Suddenly it dawned on him—it was the lack of machines. Joshi had told him and yet he had not been able to identify it immediately. It was not an entirely comforting silence. In Joshi's presence it had seemed peaceful. Juneja had never thought that he would consider the roar of a generator heartening. But here, he would have welcomed the cacophony of machines piercing through the wretched silence. It seemed to Juneja that machines showed you that you had gained in power, that you had achieved something.

Here the silence, like a vacuum, had a curious, impersonal menace to it. It wasn't directed against Juneja specifically, but it seemed like a force that was bigger and more powerful than him. It said, no, no machines here, nothing works here, nothing. Nor will you.

The three women who appeared out of nowhere frightened the hell out of him. His startled yelp petrified them as well. They had obviously seen him and had been trying to slip away unseen. Or had they been waiting to waylay him? Village belles and all that. Two were a bit long in the tooth but the third was quite hot in a crude village type of way. Also, for some reason that he couldn't quite put his finger on, she seemed familiar.

They had probably been performing their morning ablutions, thought Juneja rather fancifully. Their clothes were wet. In this sort of place there were certainly no luxurious bathrooms where womenfolk indulged in long-drawn-out baths. They'd probably had a quick dip, which didn't quite explain why they stank of shit—but that, decided Juneja, was their problem.

The women were probably off to the fields to work. Juneja asked them, hesitantly, where they were going.

They smiled at him in answer.

Juneja tried again, speaking clearly, and was more than a little startled when the oldest suddenly asked him, in perfectly serviceable Hindi, who he was.

'I am the police officer from Delhi.'

'Big police officer?'

What the fuck! To hell with modesty. 'Yes.'

'Then why have you come to such a small village?'

Why indeed! To make a buck? 'Because there is a big

problem here.' He pulled out his cigarettes again. Maybe this was real Sherlock type of detection. The devil in him made him proffer the packet to the women.

'Cigarette?'

The older women tittered in embarrassment but the younger one who had been quiet so far boldly reached out and took one. Juneja tried not to let it disturb him.

One of the women admonished her but Juneja didn't understand the broad dialect. The girl just giggled in answer and reached into her bodice to pull out a matchbox. Juneja realized it was probably the first cigarette she had ever smoked. Prior to this she must have smoked bidis.

She concentrated hard on lighting her cigarette, screwing her eyes up in concentration, and the movement jolted Juneja's memory. She was Raghu's servant girl.

'Kasturi?'

The women looked up in shock and the girl giggled again, coquettishly.

The older one spoke again, 'Yes, she is Kasturi. I am her mother and this is my sister.'

Juneja nodded. What else could he do? Shake their bloody hands?

It was a peculiar situation. On the face of it, he was in an idyllic setting—the warm sunshine, the birds, the caressing wind and three hot babes. But actually, he was in a weird village set-up with three old bats, OK, two bats and a batlet, all of whom smelt rank. *Hmm, hot.*

How do you say bye to village belles? So long? See you anon? Let's have a quick tumble?

'So, I'll be going to the house now.' *The House.*

'Wait, we wanted to ask you something.' It was the mama.

Juneja cocked an eyebrow.

'When will the road be made?'

Am I an engineer? 'I don't know. When the problems have ended.'

'The big people in Delhi have sent you?'

'Yes.' *You think I'd come here on my own?*

'So, what are the problems?'

Besides the fact that you stink? 'The problems are that—' *Nikhil, have you lost it? You want to give some biddies a progress report?*

'Why are you interested?' *That's more like it. Sajjan Kumar should have been here. He does this village bumpkin thing much better. Unfortunately, he also does the women. Just as well he isn't here.*

This time the girl spoke up. 'Obviously we are interested. The road is in our village and we should not be interested?'

The admonishment was clear this time. 'Kasturi, that is not the way to talk to a big policeman. Sahib, please forgive her. She is just a child. We are poor people.'

Juneja looked at her, bemused. The entire situation was ridiculous. The conversation, the surroundings, it was like a bad Hindi film from the eighties.

What the hell was going on?

'Were you waiting for me here?

Kasturi's mother took pity on him. 'No, no, it is nothing

like that. Yesterday, Kasturi told us about how she had seen you and so we were also curious. After all, you are a big policeman from the city.'

Was this wretched place full of capitals or was he the only one hearing them? Policeman, City, House, Family?

'So?'

'This road is very important for all of us. If there is anything we can do to help, we would be very happy to do it.'

Kasturi's derisive smile showed what she would be happy to do, but the other two seemed earnest enough.

What the fuck, Nikhil, give it a shot.

'So who is tampering with the road project materials?' he fumbled. How does one say *tamper* in Hindi?

'What materials?' asked the aunt, speaking up for the first time. Her voice was raw and cracked. This is the future, Nikhil, Sanjana would say. Quit the weed while you can. Tobacco had evidently also led to mental deficiency in this case.

'The road that is to be built here? You know?'

'Yes, but there are no road materials here.'

OK, you daft cow, I know you've never seen a road. So I'll make this nice and simple. What materials did you need for a road?

'The road ... the road that is going to be built here, you need stones and tar and machines. You understand?'

The women nodded. Even Kasturi, who'd dropped the cigarette as a bad job, looked interested.

'It is being stolen.'

'From where?' asked the mother, perturbed.

'From Arse.'

The women looked at him and at each other.

'Sahib, why would we steal the things? What would we do with them?'

The women then went on about how no one in Arse would ever do such a thing and that nobody knew where the materials were stored, and that Arse, which incidentally they pronounced to be the Butt of all things, was like this totally honest place.

Yeah. Like, totally. That was just so not true. Just like so not possible.

Juneja wondered why the entire Arse thing was making him come out all American. Wasn't Arse English? *I mean, the English call it arsehole. The Americans, asshole. Hmm. Potato, po-TAH-to. Whatever.*

But, he reflected, it *did* give him another weapon sort of thing to use against Raghu. Where were the materials being stored? Why had he not been given information about the security arrangements?

Probably, dickhead, because you didn't ask.

OK, but that idiot Gupte or Joshi or whatever should have put it in the report.

Sick of the entire damn situation, Juneja took off for the House.

The House was its usual quiet, well-behaved, majestic self, observed Juneja sourly. How come people like Muk,

Moses and this bastard Raghu have this kind of life? Clean, well maintained, tasteful. And his, Nikhil Juneja's, was a bucketful of piss that he barely managed to stay afloat in. Screeching, demanding father, a girlfriend in America who wanted him to quit smoking and cut down on his drinking, a best friend who had adopted slum children and a road scam case where non-existent road materials were being filched.

Raghu was sitting on the terrace, an elegant pair of half-moon spectacles balanced on the end of his patrician nose. Probably all the better to peruse the file balanced delicately on his knee.

The glasses added a touch of sensitivity to his otherwise outdoorsy, masculine, rugged face. Juneja felt an urgent desire to hit him viciously on his perfectly coiffed head. Why did some people have it all?

He suppressed the desire savagely. The brainless gorillas all over the place would probably beat him to pulp if he dared harm a single hair on that noggin.

'Morning, Nikhil! All well again?' Raghu gave him an over-the-glasses sophisticated look.

Juneja was a bit surprised but remembered his migraine in time. 'Yes, yes, I'm afraid it's the fresh air over here. My city lungs are more used to polluted effluences.' *Did I just use that word? Do I know what it means?*

Apparently he did, because Raghu gave an understanding laugh.

'I know what you mean. I have the same problem when I move between Cal and here.'

'Yeah, a little pollution helps clear the lungs!' Juneja demonstrated his point pithily by pulling out his cigarettes.

'Tea or a coffee to go with that?'

'Tea's good, thanks.'

One of the goons walked off to get the tea, leaving Raghu under the aegis of just one servant.

Juneja made the most of it. 'So what made you invest in Arse? Or rather when did you decide to get a piece of it?'

Raghu blinked in surprise. 'Get a piece of it? Arse, you mean?'

Yup, a piece of ass and the American action, boyo.

'I really don't see what you mean, Nikhil. Surely when and where I invest is possibly of interest to the income tax office, but I don't see why I have to tell you.'

Oh, is that how we're going to do this?

'I can see you don't, Raghu, but the Delhi Police is not your personal detective agency. We are here to investigate a crime. Independently. You tell me there is one, based on a forged report, and now I should play personal bodyguard to your investment?' *With you, for you, always.*

Raghu smiled and looked down. Juneja looked down as well. Bastard was wearing Budapester shoes. Dinckelacker, by the looks of it. Hey, but they were old. Pretty damn old. Juneja stuck out his own Timberlands. They looked new. In fact, they were pretty new. *Look at* them *over your half-moon glasses, pretty boy.*

'OK, let me put my cards on the table. After all, Nikhil, R.P. Singh Transports or Juneja Fabrics, we're all in the family business, aren't we?'

Juneja looked at him. And started laughing. It was true. What the hell was he carping about? They were on the same side of the fence.

'Nikhil, my father really wants this road project to come through. It's his dream for his native village. I guess, if the project comes through, it'll be named after him or something. Even if it isn't, it'll open up the possibility of setting up a college here and my mother's really keen on that. And that will carry our name.'

Juneja translated that into the Name.

'So, all things considered, this project is really important. For me personally, it means being able to get on with life. My dad and I haven't always seen eye to eye. Sure, after I got married and the kids came along, there was a general thaw...' Raghu smiled, only to continue ruefully, 'We've always had issues about my not taking life seriously. And I need to prove that he's wrong. You know what I mean?'

Juneja shrugged. Not really. Hell, he didn't need to prove himself to anyone.

'So, Nikhil, I won't hide anything any more. But I need your help. I need to have things work in my life now. I'm forty-five, not a young stud like you!'

Juneja looked away, embarrassed. 'No, in the police we have to keep fit. I'm hardly a stud. How did you know about Juneja Fabrics?'

'Are you kidding? Page 3 for one, and, besides, *Nikhil Juneja*! You're constantly in the news. The up-and-coming who turned his back on fortune. Also, I don't know how to say this without being crude...' Raghu paused.

Juneja who had little time for such niceties urged him to go on.

'No, man, I mean, we're not exactly poor.'

Juneja nodded. That was one way of describing their situation.

'You know, Nikhil, I thought ... I don't know if this is the right time to say it, I thought you'd understand.'

That's crude? Juneja repeated the thought out loud.

Raghu smiled. 'No, I mean, we have some ... a lot of money. And saying that is perhaps a little crude. And I thought you'd understand the problems that went with that.'

5 October 1999

Juneja appeared fresh and dewy eyed at the mansion the next day. Dinner the night before had been a home-cooked creation of Moses: shepherd's pie with a green salad that Juneja had surprisingly enjoyed. The English trifle bore no resemblance to the creamed creations of his childhood. But since there were new visitors or guests in Moses' Toes, there had been no manly chinwags. Moses had been in the kitchen and Muk had entertained the guests into believing the food was worth eight hundred bucks a head. Juneja had scurried off to enjoy some Laphroaig in peace.

He'd skipped the heavy English breakfast but the superbly brewed coffee made him feel like a quivering bloodhound. Today he'd scam the hell out of Arse!

The guards recognized him and waved his car through, but Juneja didn't have to drive far. Raghu was standing on the lawns, giving some minion the orders for the day.

'Hi, Nikhil, raring to go?'

'Absolutely. I thought you could show me the storage area today. The scene of the crime.'

Raghu paused for a second before replying, 'Sure, just give me a second to finish here.'

After some muttered consultation, they set off in Raghu's battered jeep with a flunky who had been the storeroom guard and was now doubling up as driver.

'So, how long will this project be in execution?' asked Juneja in the car.

'You know the score, Nikhil. It depends on you guys, the weather, the politicians—everything and anything.'

Juneja nodded to show his understanding of high-flying road projects.

They pulled up in front of a dilapidated ruin. Raghu identified the hills in the background as home to the famous Kali Temple of the Bloodbath of 1857. Juneja tried to look as if he cared.

'This is where you were storing the materials?' It looked like an abandoned ruin.

Juneja turned to the flunky. 'So when did you realize that material was being stolen?'

'Sahib, six months ago.'

'But you filed a report just a few weeks ago!' exclaimed Juneja.

'These things take time,' reassured Raghu.

Back to the flunky: 'So who do you suspect?'

'Sahib, local people don't want the road,' answered the fool weakly. His shifty look made Juneja pause. The women had claimed that no one was against the road.

'Which locals? Miraat? Pankot?'

'Yes, sahib, Miraat, Pankot.'

Juneja tried to harangue the fellow for more details, but Raghu intervened, muttering something about the fellow being unreliable. *Hmm, that makes sense. An unreliable guard.*

Juneja stalked up to the alleged store, as Sinha would say. It looked dilapidated. It also looked like its sole contents in the recent past had been rats.

'OK, Raghu, I'll get back to my guest house and give insurance a call. They'll make it back here by the evening and we'll take some photographs and verify the claim.'

'But you are surely as good as the insurance!'

'Raghu, I'm flattered by your faith in me, but I'm not. Besides, no insurance company will pay up without sending their guy. How much are you insured for, in any case?'

Raghu thought hard before coming up with: 'I'll have to look up the documents.'

'You don't know? Offhand, give me a figure?' The obvious discomfort made Juneja probe further.

'Look, can't we do this without the insurance people?' It was the clincher. Didn't Raghu want the theft proved? His insurance claim paid?

Turns out, no and yes.

It was a scam. A perfect scam. Raghu had got his tender bid approved by making a ridiculously low bid. He'd claimed some nonsense about wanting to give something back to his hometown. *Hmm, if you stick that up your bum, you'd have to smoke it out.*

So, his bid had been approved. Equally, it was obvious to any blind cow that he could never ever make a road or even a bloody garden path with that pathetic amount of money. So he'd insured all the road supplies and machines that he hadn't even bought.

'What do you mean? You insured stuff that you don't have?'

'Yes.'

'As in, you didn't get the supplies?'

'No, as in, they were never delivered.'

Juneja waited. Forging bills of purchase would have been easy. Raghu had probably bought the stuff over a friend or, hell, over his father's company. Juneja gave utterance to his thoughts.

No, the goods had indeed been purchased. Just the theft had been forged. And once the insurance paid up, false vouchers would be produced to show that they had been bought again and the so-called stolen goods would be pulled out of storage. So everyone was happy.

Although Raghu was visibly reluctant to put the insurance fraud in as many words, Juneja's obvious bewilderment forced him into an admission: 'There is no real theft. But for the insurance to pay, a police report has to be filed.'

'So you filed a report. And Gupte or Joshi or whoever the fuck wrote that damn report included a whole bloody paragraph about inadequate compensation.'

'Well, that was only to make sure that the insurance company bought the fact that there is indeed a problem. Since they thought it was a socio-economic problem, you know, a political issue, they suggested calling in the police first. Which is something to be grateful for because they wanted to send an expert otherwise!'

'And what should the second report say?'

'Well, theft, tampering, pilferage by person or persons unknown, would be a possibility.'

'Theft, tampering, pilferage? Because of inadequate compensation? That because the villagers are not being properly compensated by you, i.e., R.P. Singh Transports, they are stealing the materials?'

'Well, I actually have a report or a draft that you could use.'

Hmm, the first time in this entire conversation that you have said I, *my pal. Having problems with onus, are we?* 'You have a report that I can use?'

'Well, it seemed feasible to be prepared. To save you the trouble,' said Raghu, going back to non-first-person formulations.

Because that is what it was all about. Saving him, Nikhil Juneja, the trouble. But he had endured the trouble of coming here, hadn't he? Wasn't it a hardship to be stuck in Arse?

He had, and it was.

And for that hardship there would be compensation. And far from inadequate. They had agreed on the sum of sixty-seven lakhs. Just a little over sixty-five is what Juneja had demanded. It was his father's sixty-sixth birthday this year. Actually, he hadn't been sure if the sum was ridiculously low. But the only person he could have asked was his father.

Now that everything had fallen into place, the deal was finalized in no time at all. After that, there were no further problems. The money negotiations out of the way, Juneja went through 'his' report with a fine-toothed comb. God knows the insurance people and fuck knows who else would read it. No more inadequate compensation, just large-scale pilferage vaguely hinting at a rival company. Nothing anyone could do anything about. It was smooth sailing. Joshi, Gupte or whichever other local fellow wrote it did a good job and, other than change an odd phrase or two, Juneja was happy to have his work done for him.

6 October 1999

It was funny, mused Juneja, how good life could be in the boondocks. Clear skies, an open fire, crackling and giving off a sort of primeval heat. Just the colourful magnificence of the fire could hold you spellbound for hours. The kebabs tasted different out here. Fresh for one. Perhaps all this organic crap did make a difference. On the other hand, the beer came out of a bottle and still tasted pretty damn good.

He was startled out of his reverie as a stray flying spark stung his hand. But it was only a momentary lapse of peace. As usual, the silence was complete. But more than that Juneja felt the silence within himself, the well-being of his soul, yes, his soul was at peace.

Helping himself to another kebab, he mused that it was quite strange that this case—which he had not exactly been apprehensive about, nor welcomed—had turned out to be so easy.

Raghu and he had made their peace. He didn't think he'd ever warm up completely to him, but that was probably because, well, because Raghu had everything and it's difficult to like people who have everything.

But now that he, Nikhil Juneja, was going to have more than a little part of that everything, it was going to be a lot easier to like Raghu.

And here they were now. Celebrating the end of the case. Raghu was supervising some special smoked deer recipe for tonight's barbeque. The fire was burning. Juneja was drinking. Moses and Muk were about to join them. The snail was on the thorn; all was right with the world.

'You doing good, Nikhil? I can't see your glass from here.'

'It's empty but I think I'll wait till the guys come before I have another. It'll be a shame if I went to sleep on your smoked deer!'

'Have a look at it!'

Juneja hauled himself up and went over to admire Raghu's masterpiece. It was a huge carcass and unlike most things dead, smelt divine.

'Hopefully those buggers will be here soon. Otherwise I can't guarantee they'll get anything,' joked Juneja.

'Buggers is right! I don't know why I'm being polite to them after they tipped you off on to the entire thing!'

Juneja looked askance at Raghu. The humour in that statement had been decidedly forced. 'What d'you mean, Raghu?'

'C'mon, Nikhil, they told you about the road materials.'

Knowing that not just he, but also Muk and Moses were on decidedly thin ice in Arse, Juneja tried to make amends. 'Well, they didn't tell me much. I'd have cottoned on—'

'I know, Nikhil, you're nobody's fool, and I knew it right after I met you that we'd bond. But you know I stuck my neck out for those fags. My father thinks they're cousins!'

'And they know that. And they didn't tell me much. It was my investigations that helped me, you know, talking with the locals.'

'Is that a talking or a smoking deer?' It was Moses with Muk trailing in on his heels.

'It told me it smoked,' answered Juneja, grateful for their timely arrival. Time to feast.

Since Muk was stupid enough to be a teetotaller, Moses and Juneja got completely and utterly smashed. Muk was decidedly curt with both of them during the car ride home but Juneja was beyond it. Besides, since when were non-alcoholic faggots competent judges of character?

He was about to lean over and say this to Moses, who was sitting quietly abashed in his corner, but remembered his gay and retiring nature just in time.

'Man, I need to sleep this off something bad! Night, night folks!' Juneja sauntered off with a cheerful wave, spoilt only by a quick drunken stumble. Since it was over the threshold of his own bedroom, it didn't matter very much.

He wondered whether a quick nip at the remaining Laphroaig was a good idea but decided against it. A quick check of his nether regions informed him that there was no pleasure to be had in those quarters either.

Might as well hit the sack. Seems to be true: all booze and no play make me a sleepy boy.

7 October 1999

The thunderous pounding on the door made him sit up with a start. His mouth was dry and his head was pounding in tandem with the hammering the door was taking. It was Muk.

'What is it?' asked Juneja, too bewildered and fogged to be angry. 'It can't be morning!'

'It's five o'clock,' answered Muk. 'I had to get up early to start breakfast. Moses isn't feeling well.' The last was said in decidedly terse tones.

'And you wanted company?' Juneja was incredulous. This was beyond being gay.

'Are you stupid or still drunk?'

Juneja was too taken aback to answer, but Muk visibly tried to control himself. 'Look, I'm sorry. Moses … but well, never mind, that's my problem. I came to tell you that there was a message from your father last night. He wanted you to call back immediately. In fact, the message says at whatever time of night. But since we got back in so late last night, I got the message right now. So I thought I'd better wake you up.'

Juneja swallowed. 'Can I use your landline?'

'Yes, of course you can. But you might want to put on some clothes. It's rather chilly at this time.'

Juneja turned to pull on the trousers lying on the floor from last night. His head was beginning to do a serious tap dance. He left Muk at the door to go to the bathroom to sluice his face with some cold water.

As they went into Muk's office, Juneja turned to Muk. 'Could I have some coffee or tea or is it too early?'

'No, not at all. What will you have?'

'Tetley.'

He picked up the phone gingerly, not daring to guess what he would hear at the other end. His father had obviously been sitting next to the phone. It rang just twice before he heard the familiar voice.

'Nikhil?'

'Yes, it's me. What's wrong? Have you been waiting for my call?'

'Yes.' He heard his father exhale noisily and in that moment he knew.

He had set off immediately, which hadn't been hard. Muk had helped him pack. There hadn't been much. During the time he'd showered, Muk had prepared breakfast and kept all the bills ready.

He refused to eat, signing the bills with a flourish while his brain refused to make sense of all the figures.

'You have to eat. You've got too much alcohol inside you. How will you drive?'

'I will.'

'Look, just wait for ten minutes. Raghu will send over a chap. I've already called the house.'

Juneja picked up a toast to make Muk stop fluttering. 'Thanks, Muk, it's very decent of you but I'll be fine. Can you just give me a thermos of coffee or tea? I'll return it—' he stopped. *Yes, how will you return it? Planning on coming back, Arsehole?*

'Just add it to my bill.'

Muk waved an airy hand and went off with a distracted look to get the thermos and ten minutes later Juneja was speeding off.

The drive was a nightmare and later he would only have a recollection of driving like a bat out of hell, and honking, screeching vehicles protesting against his unorthodox approach.

He halted once to throw up and couldn't decide if it was the alcohol or the upheaval in his heart.

He sped on, narrowly missing a cow sitting in the middle of the road. Maybe he should have called Sajjan Kumar and asked him to drive. The man possessed the delicate touch of a tank and would surely have got him home in time. No sooner had he articulated the thought than he was forced to repudiate it.

But Nikhil, you can't be on time any more. She died yesterday, when you were drinking and pigging out on smoked deer, remember?

The recollection made him heave again. He spat sour, yellow bile out of the window without stopping the car, uncaring about who or what he may be spitting on.

Or had she died when he'd been hoping for a quick self-fondle? Mounting hysteria made him shudder and the car almost slipped out of his control. He forced himself to pull over and poured himself a cup from the thermos. The brown liquid was scalding and he was glad of the blisters that formed almost immediately on his palate. The pain made him focus.

Focus on the fact that he was going back to Delhi, where his grandmother lay dead. Soon, as per Hindu rites, his father would symbolically crack open her skull so that her spirit could leave. After that they would set fire to her. It was no use saying it was only her corpse—it was *her* and he would stand by and watch her burn.

His guardian angel was looking out for him and made him go home first. Diwan Singh had obviously left the day before and the flat was gloomy in its silence.

Juneja dropped the vomit-stained clothes and dove into the shower. The geyser had been off and the water was cold. He held it out as long as he could and then forced himself to shave. There was no point hurrying the entire thing.

As soon as he had passed Miraat, his cell phone had started beeping all the missed calls and SMSes. He'd look at them later. Sanjana was bound to be there somewhere, but he couldn't be bothered. The answering machine was also beeping red but Diwan Singh would have checked it at regular intervals, so it couldn't be anything urgent.

A cup of coffee? Or is tea a better option?

Nikhil, you are in a hurry, you know.

I know, I know.

Aftershave?

Maybe not.

He caught a glimpse of himself in the mirror and stopped again. Maybe his clothes (white kurta pajama) were too designer funeral? Would his father approve of it more if he appeared in, say, trousers and a shirt?

He decided to smoke one last cigarette on the balcony before he left.

Diwali was in a month's time and crackers and the soon-to-be-ubiquitous colourful wrapping paper that the confectioners used were beginning to make an appearance. Though today was a Thursday, some wretched blighters had not gone to school. Instead, they were on the roof, setting off rockets and 'bombs'. Vegetable vendors were beginning to go around the neighbourhood with their pushcarts. He could hear the odd servant cry out, telling the man to stop, or the lady of the house shouting back to the vendor that she didn't need vegetables that day.

Although his house was quite removed from the main road, and the kind of truck traffic he'd encountered on the highway was not allowed to enter Delhi at this time, he felt deafened by the noise. The cars, scooters and buses honking on the distant main road seemed to echo in his head. Screaming, shouting, demanding his attention. His thoughts tried to follow orderly lanes but they jostled against one another. And since it was his third chain-smoked cigarette, he was getting a tobacco high and feeling sick.

He put the cigarette out and forced himself to go in and drink a glass of water. After that there really wasn't any other excuse he could think of and had to make himself leave.

He was just about to enter the car when he remembered that Gupta would also be there, not exacty waiting for the report, but there was no harm showing a little earnestness, right? He sprinted back and picked up *the* report.

It wasn't all that bad; and as the day progressed, Juneja found himself feeling better and better.

When he arrived, the house was sombre and quiet. It was barely nine o'clock. His father had obviously been awake since the beginning of time and sitting in the drawing room. A small number of sycophants, company executives, uncles and aunties had already invaded the house. Khurana, the head of the police morgue and an old friend of his father, was sitting in one corner. He'd probably been the first person his father had called.

As he entered the room his father got up and the room fell silent. It was a bit like Amitabh Bachchan making an entry in an eighties' film. When they embraced—which in itself was weird—the entire room looked on, spellbound, and Juneja half expected them to applaud at the end.

Juneja gave a self-effacing, my-beloved-grandmother-has-just-died-and-I-know-nothing-about-it smile to the gathered audience and sat down next to Khurana.

Khurana did not disappoint. Neither did he greet or commiserate with Juneja. Par for the course.

His report was dry and concise. 'Your father called me last night at around ten o'clock. She was having respiratory problems and was on oxygen, but by the time I arrived, she was going into coronary failure.'

'So what did you do?'

Khurana smiled. 'Nikhil, my boy, there was nothing I could do. She had a long, fulfilling life. The body cannot perform forever. It is a beautiful and complex machine but it is not inexhaustible. After some time, parts get worn out. Some can be replaced, some can't. Come on, pay your last respects before the entire rigmarole starts.'

Khurana got up, leaving Juneja to follow him.

Utterly unprepared for this eventuality, Juneja was bemused by the sight of his grandmother. Whoever said death doesn't diminish had clearly never seen a dead body before. Juneja had never seen the dead body of someone he'd personally known.

She looked like a little doll. An old woman wrapped up, like a child would a doll.

Without really knowing what he was doing, he dropped down next to her on the floor. And took her hand. That it would be cold, he'd expected, but not that her nails would be blue.

'Cyanosis,' answered Khurana without waiting for the question.

The little blue hands made her seem more childlike. Juneja closed his eyes and found himself praying for her soul. He wasn't sure it existed, but it surely wasn't there in this little body. If it had existed, it had been a good, pure soul. Juneja prayed that it would find kindness and mercy.

'Come, Nikhil, your father needs your support now. The nurse will supervise the preparation of the body here.'

Prepare the body? Whose body? You mean my grandmother's? My grandmother who is now a body? Just a body? Juneja wanted to ask and then realized he had in fact spoken out loud. Pretty damn loud, considering the way Khurana was looking at him.

Khurana answered him without a trace of anger, 'Nikhil, I am sorry. I wasn't meaning to be insensitive. She was not covered because your father knew you would want to say goodbye. But the funeral is scheduled for eleven o'clock and she has to be prepared.'

'How do you prepare her?'

'She has been washed and changed. And now she will be covered and purified.'

'With what?'

'Nikhil, the priest will do it with water from the Ganga. In fact he is already here, waiting to begin.'

Juneja couldn't reason with the rising panic in him. He wanted to run away and hide; pretend this entire thing had never happened. Khurana seemed to realize this and more or less dragged him out of the room and took him into the kitchen. The sight of Diwan Singh looking as grumpy as ever helped.

'Tea,' commanded Khurana, 'sweet tea. Yes, the one you make for yourself. And you people had better start making tea for a few hundred people. Fill up all the thermos flasks.'

Juneja sat sipping the tea, trying to collect his thoughts. His father needed him. Khurana was being good to him. Judging by Diwan Singh's face, he too was concerned about him.

Could life *be* any better?

Since it had been clear that she would not survive the night, Khurana had managed to put in obituary notices in all the major dailies late last night. Juneja had a quick look at one of them. It was a quarter-page obituary. Must have cost a packet. But his father was hardly one to stint on something like this.

The photograph was from her passport but she looked kindly as ever. Juneja was a bit stunned to see his own name under his father's.

'You are a part of this family, Nikhil,' was Khurana's reassuring answer.

And as a part of that family, he now had to receive all the people who had started pouring in. As he started the greeting, the acceptance of condolences, the eternal repetition of the story (last night, heart failure around midnight, his own failure to make it on time, the daredevil drive back to Delhi, his determination to make it back for the funeral) he actually felt himself becoming a part of the family. This was perhaps where he belonged.

By ten o'clock he had started giving little details, imagined and real (cyanosis—no one asked what it meant, the truck traffic on the way back, his intuition in Arse that something was wrong). It became easier and easier.

Gupta appeared—my boy, my-boy-who-can-look-into-the-future crap. Juneja took the opportunity to press Raghu's prefabricated report into his hands. Even in the face of death, he was a true professional. If *this* didn't get him promoted, nothing else could. Gupta reciprocated by granting ten days' leave on compassionate grounds. *Hmm, others get three or four days. I* am *going places.*

Rajiv called. He couldn't get off work. Of course his parents would come for the funeral. But all of them would be there for the condolence meeting on Sunday. If there was anything, anything at all Uncle or he, Nikhil, needed, they had only to say so. Juneja had made the appropriate noises. It was amazing. It was a wonder. The entire unpleasantness was forgotten. How cool was that?

It became cooler when Sanjana called. 'Nikhil, are you OK? I'm so sorry. When Sonia showed me the papers—'

'Showed you the papers? Are you here?'

'Yes, of course I am. I've been trying to call you for the last three days but your number has been out of bounds. I was getting totally desperate!'

Juneja translated that into 'livid', but death the great leveller had put paid to that as well. Anger, jealousy et al magically became 'desperation' when people died. *Cool.*

He could get used to this. Might take some arranging, though.

'My cousin is getting married on the fourteenth and I got a cheap flight, so I decided to make it. Are you OK? Is Uncle OK? How is he taking it?' Sanjana rabbitted on.

Juneja understood this to mean his father, who had never laid eyes on Sanjana.

'It's very hard on him. I'm OK. I have to be!' *Brooding macho man, darling.*

'Is there a chauttha or any other ceremony?'

'Well, it's not exactly a chauttha though we are having it four days after her death. On Sunday morning at ten o'clock. My father doesn't want any religious affair. So it'll be a condolence meeting. An old family friend will be singing my grandmother's favourite hymns.'

Khurana's wife had volunteered to do the honours.

'Nikhil, is it OK if I make it only on Sunday? I'm already in Panipat at my uncle's place.'

So she had been livid. Already in Panipat, indeed.

'When did you get here?'

'Three days back. But—'

Time for the Juneja cut. 'Look, it's up to you. There's no pressure. At all. I mean you have a family thing to do and I understand that completely. So just get in touch if you do happen to make it to Delhi, OK?'

That if *was a nice touch, Nikhil. Light and easy.*

'Nikhil, of course I'm going to make it to Delhi. I need to talk to you. About us.'

Us. Ugh. 'Sanjana, I'm sorry, I really have to go. We're leaving for the cremation grounds.'

It wasn't even an excuse.

'Bye, Nikhil. Remember, I'm thinking of you all the time.'

And I'm thinking of your breasts. Most of the time. 'Bye.'

Why not? Maybe it was a good idea. Get her to meet Daddy-O on Sunday. He could hardly bite her head off there, at a funeral. He could, however, give him flak for not introducing the booby tramp to his grandmother. Dying wish and all that.

Booby tramp? Man, Nikhil, that is so uncool. She's your to-be and all that. Perhaps she shouldn't be, if you think of her as a booby tramp.

'Nikhil, my boy, we are all here for you. You don't have to stand alone in a corner looking so sad. She was a great lady but life comes to an end.'

Juneja nodded at the kindly uncle and escorted him to a waiting car.

The drive to the cremation grounds was nothing short of a nightmare. The pre-Diwali rush had started. There were people everywhere, and the traffic was vile. It was hard to believe that there could be death in Delhi. The streets were loud and vibrant, screaming their defiance of death and disease. The beggars hoisting their deformities at the crossings were an affirmation of life rather than of decay. They seemed to say that this, yes, this too can live, can survive. That his grandmother was dead, that the vehicle in front of his blazing red Lancer was a hearse, commanded no respect. They gathered round the car, hands cupped in supplication.

Should death make him more generous? It was hard to suppress the desire to hit a snotty-nosed child, pressing its lousy head against the window. Bastard was sky-high on smack. If he was in a police jeep, they'd dare not behave like this.

At the cremation grounds the administration of death stifled any emotional outpouring. Death certificates and bundles of cash were stamped and pocketed respectively. Now and then, you saw an occasional mourner weeping but for most people it seemed a social gathering like any other.

'Long time, no see.'

'Yes, we must meet up more often!'

Well, you won't be seeing the fucker you're leaving here again. Ever.

Juneja turned to Khurana, 'Hindu rites?'

'Your grandmother was a Hindu, not a Sikh. Your father promised her that he would bring her to this pyre.'

Juneja looked away. Was he really a part of this family?

The wood had already been heaped in a cursory pile. Obviously, the arrangements for the quantity of wood, the kind of wood and the amount of butter and oil to be used had all been made.

That small wrapped-up doll was laid on the wood. Juneja watched intently as they started putting wood on the body. It was easier to think of it as a body and not his grandmother now. The twigs that they were shoving on her face must hurt. But it was the thick log that almost crushed her and shielded her from sight which made him gulp.

His father was handed a flaming torch with which he lit the pyre. Despite the oil and butter that had been poured on the wood, there was no sudden flaming inferno. Instead, it seemed as if the flames were reluctant to reduce their fragile burden to ash. His father circled the slow smouldering pyre, pouring in oil from a long-stemmed spoon on the command of the priest. At the end of every burning verse, another spoon was added. And then his father pressed the spoon into Juneja's hand so that he too could contribute his tuppenny worth to the conflagration.

The masses of people at home were an anticlimax. But after the song-and-dance party at the cremation grounds, anything would be an anticlimax. The endless stream of visitors, of inanities and platitudes, of rites and rituals bore him home and kept him going till the evening. The funeral had turned into a social gathering. Juneja found himself promising a long-forgotten aunt that he would come over for Diwali. Not that they would be celebrating this year, what with it being a year of mourning and all that. But he would come over so that they could be together. He exchanged mobile numbers with a cousin. They'd get together for a drink. Rajiv came by at about five o'clock. His parents had come for the funeral but he had wanted to see Juneja for himself.

'I'm sorry, man, I know she really mattered to you.'

Juneja had nodded solemnly. *Had she?*

By seven o'clock, Juneja found himself hideously tired. He could barely keep his eyes open. An old family retainer had told him that a room had already been prepared for him. Just as he was beginning to feel that he'd fall asleep standing, his father said, 'Nikhil, tomorrow will also be a long day. I suggest you go to bed now and we'll talk in the morning.'

Barely able to answer, he tottered off, wondering if he could sneak a gulp of Scotch from somewhere. Diwan Singh had obviously been sent on a clothing mission and Juneja found a pair of shorts and a t-shirt on the bed as well as a change of clothes for the next day in his cupboard. His father liked doing things properly. If he wasn't careful, he'd be moving back in at the end of the week.

A quick shower had the unexpected effect of rejuvenating him. He was feeling distinctly hungry and was wondering how to get some food when he remembered that his father had had an internal telephone installed in the house for his grandmother, should she need help in any room. He picked up the phone and called the kitchen and demanded that food be sent to his room.

Diwan Singh appeared, looking more taciturn than ever.

'What's the problem?' asked Juneja, digging into the food. It was vegetarian fare but what the hell.

'There is no TV in the kitchen,' answered Diwan Singh, as if that explained everything.

'So?'

Diwan Singh refused to answer. He turned his back on Juneja and started picking up the clothes lying scattered on the ground.

Juneja took pity on him. 'Is there some pooja on?'

Diwan Singh didn't trust himself to speak. He gave Juneja a filthy look and continued folding the clothes.

'Well, I think we'll both need some more clothes tomorrow.'

Diwan Singh failed to understand. 'I have already arranged to go over and get fresh clothes.'

'I will take you home,' explained Juneja kindly, 'and then we can also pick up the small portable TV from the kitchen.'

Diwan Singh stood rooted to the spot and then nodded his head vigorously.

'Alright, then.'

Overcome with emotion, Diwan Singh asked, 'Do you want more food?'

'No, it's foul. Tomorrow we'll pick up some kebabs or something as well and then you can make them for me. Can you get me some whisky or something?'

It seemed a fair exchange. To each his own kind of spirits.

Diwan Singh evidently was not quite of the same opinion but then his desire to abase himself in front of the gods that be made him give Juneja a long, slow nod.

Fifteen minutes later, Juneja reverentially cracked open his father's Balvenie.

Diwan Singh's morals were unfortunately not completely loose. The kebabs would have to be eaten outside the house. His voice brooked no opposition and Juneja gave in gracefully and wished him a good night's sleep.

He packed away the bottle in the cupboard for the morrow. His father's taste in alcohol, at least, was above reproach. He picked up his cell phone to put in an alarm for the morning and discovered an SMS from Sanjana.

Thinking of u, love u.

Screw u, was his last coherent thought.

Well rested after a Balvenie-induced sleep, Juneja made it a point to shave in the morning. Twice. Even though they were crappy disposable razors. His father could raise hell about slovenliness. Best not to irritate him. He'd be meeting Her Boobiness in a couple of days and Juneja wanted to be taken seriously in his choice of mate and wife. Yup, although the utterance hurt, he'd decided. *Wife she would be. Become. Whatever.*

8 October 1999

The breakfast table was laid. Porridge and strange vegetarian gloop were on offer. Eggs? No, no, no.

No matter, thought Juneja, mentally planning the kebab feast of the day. He took a spoonful of the gloop and told the attending servant to get him some fresh tea. It was eight o'clock.

Diwan Singh entered looking triumphant. 'I have put the dirty clothes in the car. When will we leave?'

'Who is leaving?' It was his cat-footed father.

'I wanted to go home and pick up some stuff.'

'Surely the driver can do it. Diwan Singh can go with him.'

Diwan Singh smirked.

'I thought I would be here for some time and so tell the newspaper fellow and the milkman, as well as the guy who does the car—' Juneja found himself babbling in his desperation.

'I must say, Nikhil, I had no idea you were so well organized. I must congratulate you on your well-run household.'

Unable to decide whether this was sarcasm or praise, Juneja gave a nervous smile and studied his gloop.

'By all means, go. In fact, I would suggest that you move in here for, say, three or four weeks. There is a lot to discuss.'

'What?'

'Why don't you go pack up and then we can discuss it? If it is not to your liking, well, then you need not unpack, alright?'

Juneja nodded. At least he was spared the gloop.

Juneja was to remember that as being the only blessing of that godforsaken day. The day things changed.

They left the house at around ten o'clock and were battling the traffic as usual when Juneja's mobile rang. It was impossible to pick it up and he didn't even try. He did glance at the display, though, to make sure it wasn't Sanjana—it didn't pay to play too hard to get. It was a Delhi number, but not one he recognized. He'd call later. But then the phone rang again. Juneja had just pulled up at a red light and decided to take the call.

'Additional Commissioner Juneja?'

Juneja recognized the voice immediately. Well, not the owner, but the Voice. It had to be a flunkey policeman from somewhere. Nobody else managed that mix of subservience and insult the way the police did.

'Speaking. Who is this?'

'Sir, Inspector Madanlal Sharma from Bahadurgarh station, sir.' Madanlal Sharma dropped the insulting tone rapidly. Like Juneja, he too recognized the Voice.

'Sir, I have here a Mr Schuwelbaum, sir, who is very much wanting to talk to you.'

The light turned green and Juneja found himself needing a third hand to change the gear.

'I'll call back.'

'No, sir—'

Juneja cut off the squawking voice. *Stupid fool.*

Diwan Singh gave him a questioning look.

'Work,' explained Juneja, laconically.

The mobile started ringing again. Juneja shook his head. This was ridiculous. He picked up the phone and barked into it, 'Wait.'

Desisting from mouthing obscenities for fear of irritating Diwan Singh, he pulled over. He was going to tee off Madanlal Sharma's balls.

But first he needed to get rid of Diwan Singh.

'Get me some cigarettes,' he said, 'I'll finish the call in the meantime.'

Diwan Singh nodded his assent and left as Juneja picked up the mobile again.

'What the fuck is going on? How dare you call me up like this? Are you mad?'

Unable to interject an answer in the face of Juneja's vitriol, Madanlal Sharma grovelled, 'Sir, very sorry, sir. Very sorry. But, sir, but this is an emergency. That is what Mr Schuwelbaum is saying.'

'Who is Mr Fucking Schuwelbaum?'

The question immediately bolstered Madanlal Sharma's confidence.

'One second, sir, please hold.'

Juneja then heard him bellow, 'Hey asshole Schuwelbaum, Juneja Sir doesn't even *know* who you are! Emergency! Even when I fuck your mother, it won't be an emergency!'

He could hear faint, cultured tones in the background object to this form of familiarity. Did he know Schuwelbaum?

'Sharma? Sharma, put this Schuwelbaum on.'

'Sir? You want me to give him phone?'

'Yes.'

'Here, Schuwelbaum, talk to Juneja Sir.'

'Nikhil?'

It was a moment of clarity. Nikhil. Schuwelbaum knew him?

'Yes. Who the hell is this?'

'Nikhil, it's me, me, Moses from Arse.'

Funny, thought Juneja, he pronounced it Arse. Like a bum. But that thought was rapidly pushed away as Moses continued, 'Nikhil, you have to come here. Please, it's a matter of life and death. They won't write down the report and Nikhil, I can't take her back. They'll kill me.'

'Moses? What are you talking about? Has something happened to Muk?'

'Muk? No, no—' His voice was abruptly cut off and Madanlal Sharma's unctuous tones filled Juneja's ear once more, 'Sir, is this gentleman your friend? Sir, we have not refused to write report, but there are political considerations, sir.'

So, there was a major problem. The wretched men had probably been caught having it off and then been hassled by some wretched policeman. Obviously, Moses must have throught nothing about walking into the police station to complain about the infringement of his rights; the police station would have refused to lodge a complaint about another policeman.

Hmm, but he was at the Bahadurgarh *station. Muk had probably been able to persuade Moses not to walk into the Miraat station and complain about their colleague.*

'Wait, Sharma, just shut up. Listen, you give Mr Schuwelbaum some tea and I will call you back, OK? No playing with him. Do you understand me?'

'Yes, sir.'

Juneja cut the phone off and stared into the distance, absent-mindedly lighting a cigarette.

Moses in trouble. The bastard should thank the colour of his skin that Madanlal Sharma had even bothered calling me.

Diwan Singh's reappearance jolted Juneja. What was to be done now?

'What are we doing now?' asked Diwan Singh, correctly reading Juneja's thoughts.

'I don't know. There's an emergency. Look, we're quite close to the station. Let me see what's going on and then we can go home, alright?'

Diwan Singh nodded his assent. The wretched TV programme was in the evening. What did he care?

Juneja drove through the traffic slower than usual, in no hurry to get to the station. *How is this problem to be solved? Think, Nikhil, think. Moses, white, Muk, Indian. Arse small, Raghu in your pocket, Arse in Raghu's pocket. That could be the lever.*

Go to Arse, talk to Raghu and get the problem sorted out. Also beat the crap out of Gupte or Joshi or whichever donkey had been stupid enough to screw over Moses.

Then why bother going to the station? U-turn and go back down the road and drive out of Delhi to get the bypass via Gurgaon.

That made a lot more sense.

Just as he pulled through the cut under the bridge, Juneja saw a familiar figure sitting in a police jeep under a tree.

'Sajjan Kumar? What are you doing here?'

'Sir, Gupta Sir has said I have to wait till the inquiry.' Correctly understanding that to mean that Sajjan Kumar had been given the boot from the station to avoid bad press and was hanging around the traffic beat to make some money off the beggars, Juneja scowled in concentration. The entire thing was falling into place.

Take Sajjan Kumar to Arse. Let him drive for one, let him beat up whichever asshole needed beating up for another. Return triumphant to Delhi, accompanied by Sajjan Kumar of Team Juneja, shining brightly in a foreigner-friendly case. Even better, a foreigner-friendly, gay case. Delhi Police, the stuff gay, white dreams are made of.

Diwan Singh sulked a bit, but Juneja assured him that they'd be back by the evening. That Sajjan Kumar was deeply respectful to Diwan Singh was an additional factor. Juneja had told him that Diwan Singh was addicted to devotional channels, much like Sajjan Kumar's own mother. After some time, Diwan Singh, who was sitting in front with Sajjan Kumar, thawed a little and even discussed the pros and cons of the different channels with Sajjan Kumar.

Lounging at the back with a cigarette, Juneja listened to their conversation with half an ear. It was strange to think that Sajjan Kumar and Diwan Singh had religion in common. Did they also have sex in common? Was Diwan Singh's conservative veneer a façade for violent sex? The thought disturbed Juneja so much that he immediately picked up his cell phone and started composing an SMS to Sanjana.

C u at 10 on d 10th at chauttha. Luv u. N.

Hmm. Did he indeed *luv* her? Perhaps, instead of wasting his time and energy thinking about Diwan Singh's member, he should think about his own. Life had certainly improved after Sanjana. When she wasn't in America, he had company, and sex. OK, Rajiv and Geetu didn't like her very much but then after what had happened with them, perhaps that wasn't all that important. Would Big Daddy-O like her? Probably. And he, Nikhil Juneja, would live happily ever after. That was really the crux of the entire thing.

Ready to put in your papers, hang up your boots and sign up for matrimony and patrimony in one fell swoop, Nikhil? Say bye-bye to the world of bachelor parties and hello to Swunny and Dhwunny.

Maybe it doesn't have to be that way. Maybe he could have a cool, swinging kind of marriage, where they listened to jazz and ate Thai food on the weekends. Went on trekking holidays and drank wine. Had real records of Kishori Amonkar and Duke Ellington instead of CDs of Daler Mehendi and Anup Jalota. Maybe instead of living with

Daddy, they would have a cool apartment and weekend retreats. Fabindia furnishings. Jute carpeting. Teak lamps. Jamini Roy prints. The list of required accoutrements for an alternative lifestyle was endless. And also cringe inducing and sickening.

He looked out of the window. They were gradually leaving the city. Some pathetic sorts of villages were emerging, interspersed with huge industrial chimneys. Like life in Arse. Sandwiched between Pankot and Miraat. Between India past and present. An autocracy in a democracy.

Was that possible?

Was it possible to be democratic in an autocratic set-up? Was Raghu the benevolent dictator he made out to be? Was his father the kind, nice man *he* made out to be?

'Sir?'

It was Sajjan Kumar.

'What?'

'We stop for latrine?'

'Yes.'

Was another response possible? Only a dictator would dictate to another man's bladder. He, Nikhil Juneja, was certainly not a despot or a dictator and as such when his minions wanted to go to the toilet, they said so and they went. It wasn't even really a question of granting permission. But surely good manners decreed that you announce the intention to urinate?

Sajjan Kumar pulled over near a roadside shack, clearly announcing his intentions to take more than a leak.

Diwan Singh and Juneja too tottered out.

'Sajjan Kumar, find out about tea and maybe something to eat.'

It was a typical dhaba. Small, blackened with years of use and lack of hygiene and cleanliness. It must be hell in summer. In October, it was just about bearable. The trucks roaring past ensured a steady supply of dust that had worked its way into every available surface.

The plastic chair that Juneja pulled over was caked with dirt, its red colour reduced to a dull brown. Juneja capriciously scraped away a nailful of dirt to see the real colour—an action he regretted immediately. How was he going to get his nail clean now?

Sajjan Kumar went into the shack to bellow their order and then sauntered off behind the shack. To the latrine, assumed Juneja, lighting up yet another cigarette. He was feeling light-headed from the lack of food. Behind him Diwan Singh was stretching noisily.

Juneja was about to ask him what he wanted to eat when his phone rang. It was Sanjana.

'Hi!'

'Hey, what's up?'

'Nothing, I just wanted to tell you that I've been thinking about you and dreaming about you and fantasizing about you!' The last was a husky whisper.

And my father's money, while you're at it? 'And I thought you were at your cousin's wedding!'

'Nikhil, don't be like that! Have you been thinking about me?'

And it's time to score. 'My grandmother just died. I haven't had time to think about anything.' *Except your boobs. Or breasts, as I will call them in the future.*

'Oh, Nikhil, I know, and I want to be there for you.'

Where? On your knees is always a good place. 'Sweetheart, I don't know where I am myself.' From where was he picking up this nonsense? Archie's cards?

'Nikhil, I just wanted to confirm the chauttha. My parents want to pay their condolences personally. Is that OK? I mean, they've heard so much about you. But they'll understand—'

He couldn't help but cut her off. Not so fast, not so soon.

'No, Sanjana, sweetheart, please. My father is very conservative about such things and the entire ceremony is really only for the family. It's just because I told him how important you are for me that it's OK. But please don't get your parents now. Besides, I'm going to be really caught up with the arrangements and there will be nobody to, to, you know, be with them.'

Thank god, he'd scored. No way she'd accept this otherwise.

'Are you sure, Nikhil? I mean we really want to be there for you, you know.'

All of you on your knees? Hey I'm big, but not that *big.* 'Sanjana, sweetheart, it's not a question of being sure. I just don't want to upset my father right now. It's really very traumatic for him.' *And for me, by implication.*

'Nikhil, I am there for you. Whatever, whenever.'

'I know, and that is my source of strength.' *And also of endless shame.*

'I'm coming in to town tonight. Shall we meet up for a late-night coffee?'

'That sounds good. Give me a call, OK?'

'OK.'

He cut the phone before she could love him any more.

They made it to the station at one o'clock in the afternoon. Juneja was sick of the entire affair. The food at the dhaba had been lousy and his stomach was beginning to grumble. Diwan Singh, who had realized that they were going to be late getting back, was also grumbling, albeit under his breath, but loud enough for Juneja to know. Sajjan Kumar continued to be death-defyingly cheerful but then what did he know? *Bastard is probably just happy being out of Delhi.*

The station was the usual mess of pathetic policemen and apathetic applicants. Juneja ignored all of them and got himself a flunkey.

'Madanlal Sharma?'

'Sir has gone for lunch break,' answered the constable, also recognizing the tone despite the lack of uniform.

'Take me to his office and get us some Pepsi or something,' commanded Juneja. The fizz would make him burp and relieve the pressure off his straining stomach. It was either that, or risking a visit to the police latrine.

They sauntered into the office and sat down. Juneja gulped down the cola when it came and waited for the eructation. In vain.

The swing doors opened and a portly, moustached man entered.

'Madanlal Sharma?' demanded Juneja aggressively. His patience was running thin and he wanted to get back to Delhi.

'Yes, sir. Additional Commissioner Juneja, sir?'

'Yes. Where is Moses Schuwelbaum?'

'Sir, only as precautionary measure, they have been placed in the cells. I will just now go and bring the couple before you.'

So it *was* a case of buggery. Well, if nothing else, Sajjan Kumar would learn something. Or perhaps be able to teach the faggots something. Juneja was vaguely disappointed. He'd been hoping that Moses and Muk wouldn't fall into this last trap of clichéd gay behaviour. Bastards must have been having it off in the fields—a fondle in the mustard fields is worth two screws in bed. Why? What was it about the Great Outdoors that made people think horizontally? The trees? Were they also a phallic symbol, much like everything else, if Sanjana were to be believed? Were trees what gay dreams were made of?

But it was no homosexual couple that entered the room. It was a grubby, exhausted-looking Moses but instead of the muscular, rippling Muk, he was accompanied by an incredibly dirty and smelly woman. Her sari was torn. She had what appeared to be dried blood on her face, a split lip, the makings of a huge black eye, and she was limping.

Had Moses finally had enough ass and raped this woman? Surely it couldn't be illegal to screw this old bag.

'Who is this? Moses? Why did you want me here?'

The woman, as if in answer, made some pathetic effort to touch his feet but some broken, strained, screwed-up part in her prevented her from bowing too low, much to Juneja's relief.

'Namaste, sahib,' she said. Her voice was deep and sounded terribly familiar.

Juneja turned to Moses, who was looking around for a chair to collapse in, while Madanlal Sharma stood around, excavating his molars.

'Get a chair,' he commanded tersely.

But when the chair came, Moses packed the old biddy into it, who in turn tried to gracefully slide to the ground but Moses held her firmly and she subsided in a meek heap.

'Get another chair,' demanded Juneja. 'What the hell is this, Moses? What have you been up to and who the hell is this?'

But Moses was at the end of his strength and Sajjan Kumar was moved to offer him his own seat, without Juneja having to tell him to do so.

Juneja turned to Madanlal Sharma, who had returned with two folding chairs. 'Get some Pepsi, something to eat, snacks, something ...' He trailed off.

What was going on?

They sat in an uncomfortable silence. Moses seemed content to lie with his eyes closed. The biddy had pulled up her legs and was squatting awkwardly on the chair.

Diwan Singh had stopped grumbling and was looking gobsmacked by the proceedings. Was this real police work? Sajjan Kumar, who knew it was, lolled against the door frame, fingering his balls.

Juneja lit a cigarette to break the silence. Diwan Singh sniffed at the back. He took this entire no-smoking-in-public-places thing very seriously. Besides, Juneja suspected he also had some antiquated ideas about the police being upholders of the law. Then Moses started sniffing and Juneja was about to give up the cigarette as a bad idea.

'Should I put it out?'

But Moses was crying silently. The sniffs were a vain attempt not to sob.

Madanlal Sharma entered bearing a tray with four cola bottles and a plateful of rancid fried stuff. Juneja's stomach gave a discernible warning and he picked up the bottle with the air of a harried man. 'Look, Moses, whatever it is, we can sort it out. You're looking exhausted. So I suggest you eat something and ... here have something to drink. You need the sugar.'

Moses nodded, and slowly took the bottle from Juneja's hand. Juneja picked up the plate and offered it to Moses, who reluctantly took a piece of fried mush. Sajjan Kumar came forward to help himself to the free food and drink. Two bottles remained. One for him and one for Diwan Singh ... and one for the hag?

It was exquisitely embarrassing. But obviously only for Juneja. The heap on the chair had buried its face in its arms.

Should he give her a bottle? And not give Diwan Singh a bottle? No, not possible. Breach of etiquette. Give Diwan Singh a bottle and not take one himself? No. Breach of no etiquette, but not a thought worth entertaining. Not offer the heap the Pepsi? *Who* takes the last Pepsi and lets an injured, although poor and slummy-type woman die of thirst? Speaking of which, maybe she's not thirsty.

Solution: Offer her a bottle, pray she'll say no. And then all the right people will have one. If she is shameless enough to say yes, hopefully, by that time, Diwan Singh, who will have heard the entire exchange, will refuse *his* bottle. *Excellent.*

'Do you want a Pepsi?'

Silence. Moses was concentrating on the fried crap. Sajjan Kumar and Diwan Singh knew they weren't being spoken to. Madanlal Sharma looked up, startled. But the heap was impervious.

'Excuse me? Hello?' Juneja turned for help. 'Moses, what's her name?'

'It's … Actually, Nikhil, I don't know.'

'You're here with a woman you don't know?'

'She's Kasturi's mother. You know Kasturi? Raghu's servant girl?'

And that explains anything?

Well, at least he knew now why her voice had sounded familiar. It was one of the three women from the fields. That young servant girl of Raghu's and her aged female relatives.

'So ask her if she wants some Pepsi.'

'I think she'd be happier with tea,' answered Moses.

Excellent idea. Why couldn't he have thought of it himself?

He turned to Madanlal Sharma. 'Get some tea.'

'For you, sir?'

'Yes.' That meant it would be a little better than the overcooked brown bilge the teashops generally handed out.

'So why have you brought her here?' Juneja turned back to Moses, who had improved distinctly after drinking the cola.

'Nikhil, I really don't know how to say this, but something nightmarish has happened. The villagers, led by Raghu and his henchmen, attacked her yesterday. I really don't know why.'

Juneja broke in, 'Raghu attacked her? For what? Stealing?'

'No, Nikhil, for god's sake, don't talk like that!'

'OK, so why did they attack her?'

Madanlal Sharma entered at this moment. 'Sir, tea?'

'Yes, give it to her.'

Somewhat bemused, Madanlal Sharma walked up to the heap and gave her shoulder a cursory shake. The woman gave a low moan and looked up. The tea was obviously the right idea, though how she was going to drink it with those smashed lips was anyone's guess.

The gathered assembly evidently had the same thought and there was a hushed silence as the men watched her hold the cup in a fragile hand.

She looked around and then carefully placed the glass on the table next to her. Unaware of her audience, she worked her mouth as if testing it was all still there and then tried to spit into one end of her sari. But evidently her mouth was too dry. Before anyone could say or do anything, she dipped that filthy rag into the cup, and with that wet cloth she moistened and softened her lips. Then, with a sigh of pain or relief or both, she picked up the glass again and took a first careful sip.

Moses forced himself to look away and cleared his throat. 'Look, Nikhil, I really don't know what's happening. She crawled over to us yesterday evening and more or less collapsed. Muk didn't want to come. We had had something of a fight and he walked off.'

'That's convenient for you.'

'What the hell do you mean by that? What do you mean *convenient*?'

'Moses, this has nothing to do with me or with what I mean by convenient. But it is weird and highly suspicious that you come here with a battered woman who looks like she's been assaulted and you have no alibi.'

'Nikhil, you're getting this all wrong. Talk to her. She'll tell you the whole story. And Muk was there when she came. We had the fight after that.'

'What did you fight about?'

'We fought about ... Look, Nikhil, I don't want to discuss this right now.'

OK, keep your knickers on. Just a little cultural exchange, you know, what gays fight about and all that.

'So,' Juneja turned to Kasturi's mother, 'what is the problem?'

Before she could answer, he held up a hand. All this excitement was making him forget police procedure. On the other hand, filing FIRs wasn't really his job.

Juneja said to Madanlal Sharma, 'You better write this down. Moses and Diwan Singh, you're going to be witnesses to what she says. That her report was not made under pressure, etc. etc., alright?'

Diwan Singh nodded his assent, his eyes as big as saucers.

'Moses, you OK? You understand enough Hindi?'

To prove that he indeed did, Moses answered in Hindi, 'Understand big, speak small.'

The Boys in Brown exchanged meaningful glances.

Right. Then let's get on with the big understanding. 'So, what is your name?'

'Sarbati Devi.'

Juneja looked blank. But Madanlal Sharma guffawed, 'Sarbati!' And Juneja got the joke. From sherbet. Syrupy, sweet, honey. It would have been a better name for her daughter, who at least had some sort of pretensions of being beautiful. This crone was far from honeyed. But at least she was self-assured and composed, unlike that babbling faggot Moses.

'Well, Sarbati, what has happened? You came to this man's house,' he pointed at Moses, 'and said you needed help. We are here to help you and we will help you. But before we start off with your story I need to fill up a form with your details. Alright?'

She nodded her assent.

'Your name is Sarbati Devi and you are a resident of ?'

'Aarsh.'

'What is your occupation? Your work?'

'I am a cleaner, a sweeper.'

Nice one, Moses. You owe me big time. I give you Laphroaig, you give me la sweeper? 'Age?'

'Thirty-five.'

Juneja looked up, appalled. OK, her hair was black, but whose wasn't? She looked at least sixty. Perhaps he should indulge her. These illiterate types had no idea about dates or years. She probably meant fifty-three.

'Are you sure?

'My father said I was born the day Pandit Nehru died. That was the twenty-seventh of May 1964. So I became thirty-five in May.'

Juneja looked around at the gathered brethren. Could anyone verify when Nehru had died?

'You can do maths?'

'My father taught me how to read and write Hindi. He was a freedom fighter, a follower of Gandhiji. That is why I named my daughter Kasturi. After Gandhiji's wife.'

Of course, the lissome lass. He could've sworn she was at least sixteen.

So, diddle my diddle, riddle me this, 'How old is Kasturi, then?'

'She would have been seventeen this year. In November.'

Juneja sighed. Women and their theatrics.

'Alright now, from the beginning, I want you to tell me how you came to be in this condition. OK? From the beginning.'

Sarbati nodded. She picked up her cold glass of tea as if in preparation, but after a small sip she replaced it on the table.

'The beginning, sahib, is a long time ago and I don't think we have the time.'

Damn right we don't. 'So you start with who did this to you and why. Even if you or Kasturi have stolen something, broken something, it's alright. Nobody has the right to do this to you.'

Some sherbet for Moses' white ears.

'No, sahib, I haven't broken or stolen anything. In fact, that is the problem. After you left, the Big Sahib called all of us villagers to the House. We were all there. He said that the materials that were necessary to build the road were being stolen. He said that you had come to find out who was the thief and that we should help you and answer all your questions. He said that here was a thief in the village who did not want the road to be built.

'And then Kasturi said that she had not known this. So the Big Sahib asked her what she meant. And she told him how we had met you ... how we had told you that there were no thieves in Aarsh. And now that the Big Sahib had told us that there were indeed thieves, we would surely help you find them.

'But the Big Sahib became very angry. He wanted to know everything about our meeting with you. And then he said that we had insulted him and told lies to you, that we were liars and thieves, and that we should be punished.

'At that time we didn't know how they would punish us. My sister and I were very scared. We don't have much money, sahib. If the Big Sahib levies fines on us, how will we pay? I have been trying to save a little money for Kasturi's dowry but I thought that I will now have to spend it on this. I will have nothing left.

'But, sahib, we should have known. We are women. Women are punished only in one way and that is how they punished us. My sister is a widow and I never had any man, so we had no menfolk to protect us. The whole village, sahib, the whole village. There was not one man, not *one* man who would protect us. No, they only wanted to fuck us.

'I begged and pleaded with them. I told them I will make good the loss, but they should let my Kasturi go. That fat merchant, Ram Lal, he will tell you, I fell on my knees before him, I begged with him, I sucked his cock. Even though it stank I sucked it. But they only laughed and they made my Kasturi watch. They made her see what a whore her mother was, they made her see what they had in store for her.

'She was a virgin. My sister and I, we are old women. We know what animals men are, but she was a child. She kept asking me to stop. You see, I kept telling those men to fuck me, repeating how horny I was, how much sex I needed, but it was not enough for them. After the first dozen, they started beating me. They called me names and started hitting me. They whipped me with sticks and then tried to fuck me with it. But all that wasn't enough to save Kasturi.

'They pulled at her clothes like hungry rats and stripped her of her clothes. She had her period; she was bleeding, and that made them even more angry.

'Me, they had started beating only after some time, but since she was bleeding, they beat her right from the beginning. They said that she was unclean, that she wanted to defile them; that it was their kindness that they were willing to touch a lower-caste girl like her whom no decent man would even spit upon. And then they started fucking her, but they said they will not put their cock in her. So they fucked her from the back. But so that she knows what it is like to be a woman, they fucked her from the front with a broom. They said that since she is from the sweeper caste, this is what she will like.

'Sahib, the entire day, the entire day it went on. And finally when it became dark and my child's body was limp and lifeless, they left us to die.

'I don't know when I came to my senses. I crawled over to my Kasturi, but she was gone. My sister was still alive, but I could not get her to help me. She was too badly injured. She was a man, my sister. She had tried to help me. She had tried to make those men fuck her like I did. She tried to save my child. And they killed her for it.

'I told myself, I must bring my daughter's murder to justice. In that village there was no one I could turn to for help. I hid their bodies. And then I thought of the foreign sahibs. They were always kind to us. When we cleaned their house, they gave us tea. In winter, the sahib would give us warm water to clean the floor. Maybe he will help me today. And if he doesn't, it won't matter.'

So this was Raghu's little punishment. *OK, big deal, it can be dealt with. It must be dealt with.*

Juneja found himself looking for words to say. For noise to fill the silence. In desperation he looked up, away from those sherbet-y eyes.

The sounds of the police station outside of the room seeped in as if from another world. But they accentuated rather than mitigated the fact that this little room was apart and separate from all that was normal and good.

How would they, how would *he*, ever go back to that old, good world?

It was clear that before any action could be taken against any possible culprits, they had to have possession of the bodies. After that, Sarbati needed to get a medical examination. But since Sarbati was unable to explain where exactly she had hidden the bodies, it was decided that she would go back to Arse, escorted by Madanlal Sharma. They would then return with the bodies.

Meanwhile, an official FIR would be filed at this police station, which meant that Delhi could be directly in charge of the case.

Juneja put both of them into the police hearse along with two constables for extra safety and then got on to the phone to Khurana. 'I need your help.'

'Nikhil? What's wrong? Is your father alright?'

'Yes, of course. I mean, I think he's alright, I mean, this is not about him. I need your help in a medical matter.'

'What do you mean?'

'I need you to examine a woman in a rape case.'

'No, Nikhil, I will not help that thug of yours. I understand that police work is brutal and dangerous and also that the police need to be brutal in order to apprehend criminals, but I cannot and will not condone rape.'

Nice, Nikhil, now explain how it's not that thug of yours.

'No, it's not Sajjan Kumar—' *But it is Sajjan Kumar you have brought with you. It is Sajjan Kumar who has heard her story. And now it's you who is wondering if it turned him on.*

'No, this is another case. The local police station has refused to lodge an FIR because of local politics. In fact, it's a case of gang rape and murder. Two of the women have been raped, well, more or less to death.'

'Raped to death?' Khurana's tone was incredulous.

'I don't know about this stuff. I'm not a doctor!'

'Then I suggest you bring the bodies here. But Nikhil, I'm not a gynaecologist. I can't help you with the victim, I mean the living victim.'

That's a good name for her.

'But I have no one else to go to. Please, Khurana Uncle, please.'

He didn't realize until it was out that he'd let slip that

old name. The name that he'd called this man when he was literally dandled on his knee. His father always tried to get him to say Peshi Uncle, but for him he'd always been Khurana Uncle. One of the magic people who could make everything alright.

He sure as hell wasn't doing that now.

'Nikhil, I want to help you but if you want to help this woman, you must get her to a doctor whose opinion will carry weight in court. Besides, if she has been raped in this horrible fashion, she needs therapy, professional help. I'm a pathologist.'

You're one of the magic people, damn it, you have to help me.

'OK, then will you get the right doctor to the morgue?'

'Nikhil, it's five o'clock on a Friday evening. How can I get a doctor now?'

'I don't know.'

Khurana sighed. 'Alright, get here then. We'll see what can be done.'

So, Nikhil, that's out of the way. Now we wait for Sarbati to get back with her dead sister and daughter who have been mauled or beaten to death since Khurana claims that they can't have been raped to death. Wait with Diwan Singh and Sajjan Kumar. A religious freak and a sex fiend. Ask them for advice maybe. Ask Diwan Singh to pray for them, ask him if the story was true, ask him how things like this could happen.

O you inhumane God, how could you let this happen? Are you a male God? Did your dick not fall off before you let this happen? Stop, stop, maybe it's a female God, i.e., Goddess, so why did you let the chicks get raped, huh? Not getting enough yourself? Boohoo, my heart breaks for you.

Knock it off, Nikhil, this is boring crap. You're not even interested in the pathetic answers to these silly questions, assuming you'd get them.

Nope, the real questions are for Sajjan Kumar. So did the story turn you on? The hot gang-bang? Was it like that for you? Did you want white pussy or was it just a woman? Hey, just asking, just asking. Is it hot, when a woman fights? Did Theresa Schmidt fight? She must have. She had a busted lip, didn't she?

Stop it, Nikhil.

I can't. I keep seeing images I don't want to see, and keep seeing Sajjan Kumar because he's in front of me.

So get out of the room, go for a walk, call up your father, tell him you'll be late, organize some food, some coffee, get on with your life.

He was leaving the room when the cell phone rang. Thank god for distractions.

'Yes?'

'Hi, Nick?'

'Sanjana? Where are you calling from?'

'I'm in Delhi. I wanted to ask you when you'll be picking me up or should I come over to Jor Bagh?'

'Honey, I'm not in Delhi. I mean I am, but I'm more or less on the border and I'm caught up in some work and—'

'I thought we were meeting up for coffee today and you're on leave because of your grandmother's funeral, so how can you be working?'

'Sanjana, sweetheart, look, I'm up to my neck in work and I have officially taken leave, but this big case has come up,' he paused. How could he explain this to her on the telephone? 'Look, I think I'll be back before it's too late. Shall we try for coffee after dinner?'

'Nikhil, I'm staying at Sonia's place and I can't go out later. She's got people over for dinner. But you can come over, if you want to. I mean you can see me, if you want to. But if you don't then please say so, so that I don't embarrass or inconvenience you in any way by coming for the condolence ceremony for your grandmother.'

OK, after that scintillating bit of conversation, let's get that coffee organized.

There was no way in hell that they were making it back in time for dinner, let alone coffee at a decent hour. It was almost nine o'clock in the evening by the time they got to the police morgue. Khurana was patiently waiting for them, but there was a distinctly quizzical glint in his eye as he looked at Juneja.

'I will conduct the postmortem tomorrow morning. The woman you have brought with you can be examined now. I've managed to get a lady doctor to wait. She can spend the night here. I suggest you come over to the morgue by about twelve and we can discuss my findings then.'

Juneja dropped off Sajjan Kumar at a bus stop and, with superhuman effort, picked up the TV and dropped off Diwan Singh at his father's house. Not that it seemed to matter to Diwan Singh. The horrors of the day had left him too shocked to care one way or the other.

Juneja told Diwan Singh to tell his father that he would sleep in his own flat that night. It would make it easier to go over to Khurana's the next day. Diwan Singh nodded perfunctorily and walked off in a daze.

Juneja's drive back home was slow. The traffic was still heavy but the city was slowly coming to rest. He was exhausted and wide awake. The idea of an empty flat was distinctly unappealing, as was going over to Sonia's place. He found he'd gone straight at the crossing at Race Course Road instead of turning right. The Ashoka Hotel loomed large and on a whim he drove on into the diplomatic area. Here the streets were almost deserted. The embassies looked strangely bereft now that the long lines of applicants had gone home.

On the deserted roads, the car went in and out of the shadows cast by the overhead streetlights and suddenly Juneja felt as if he were transported back to a childhood long past. The drives back home after a late evening, when he would be lolling, half asleep on the backseat. The shadows would come and go, to and fro, like mini days and nights. Juneja was never quite certain if he wanted to reach home, where he could finally fall into his bed, or whether he wanted that ride home to go on endlessly, like he did today.

He stopped at a roadside stall and ate bread and eggs despite having no appetite for it. For lack of anything better to do, he drove home. The oblivion that came with sleep would stop his mind from working. He didn't sleep particularly well that night.

9 October 1999

When he got up the next day, he felt terribly disoriented. The flat was strangely still. It echoed the silent menace of Arse.

Knock it off, Nikhil, it's just that Diwan Singh isn't there. Shower, fix yourself some breakfast and get going.

The bathroom was dusty and he'd forgotten to turn on the geyser the night before. So the water was stone cold.

He sat down in the drawing room with a cup of instant coffee and a cigarette. He had no desire to read the newspaper. In fact, the apartment was altogether rather uncomfortable. Sanjana had been appalled that his décor consisted of alcohol—bottles of booze placed, quite aesthetically, with spot lighting . He'd tried to convince her that that was all the people he ever invited were interested in. But her take was that it wasn't 'warm enough'. Warmth apparently radiated from colour. If you covered the walls and a mattress on the ground with some bilious yellow and green muck which bled every time it was washed, then you were very warm. And caring. As far as he was concerned, it meant Sanjana slept over and that translated into warmth in his bed. And he took care of that. It also meant that all his socks and vests had a yellow and green tinge. Yellow and green—the colours of vomit *and* wild, animal sex? Who'd have thought!

He glanced desultorily at his watch and discovered that it was already ten o'clock.

Time he left to meet Khurana. Would the story of the wild sex make him vomit? If it did, he was definitely going to change the colour scheme of the drawing room, no matter what Sanjana said.

'Nikhil, come in, come in! I'm glad that you are so punctual. I've just finished, or at least done all that I can do at this stage. Shall we talk first?'

Juneja nodded his assent.

Khurana had made Madanlal Sharma drive the hearse to the morgue and had deigned to be present when the bodies were unloaded. Juneja himself had left before the bodies were brought in.

Women who'd been screwed to death were bound to look weird. Not that Juneja hadn't seen raped women before. Working with Sajjan Kumar meant it was an occupational hazard. But still, this was different. It was. He wasn't sure why or how, but it was.

'Tea?'

'Thank you,' responded Juneja. Khurana drank fairy tea—light, fragrant stuff. It probably had a calming effect on the stomach.

After an initial sip, Juneja felt emboldened enough to set the ball rolling. 'So what did they die of?'

Khurana looked at him with raised eyebrows. 'What do you mean? Of cardiac arrest, naturally! Or at least the younger one did. In the case of the older woman, she had been subjected to physical torture. There must have been severe loss of blood. In fact, the place, the *area* rather, where she was found must have been covered with blood.'

Juneja blanched.

'Yes, Nikhil, it is a horrifying crime. It's not just the fact of the women being raped, to death, as you say. It's horrifying when you imagine that another human being did this ... that this crime was done by men like you and me.'

Juneja studied his feet. *He* hadn't done it.

'How come the old one survived?' It was the question he'd spent the night wrestling with. Hadn't she wanted to die?

'What precisely do you mean by *how*?'

'Weren't her injuries bad?'

'Obviously not bad enough, Nikhil! I don't understand what you mean.'

'Wasn't she raped badly?'

'Yes, there is severe vaginal bruising and some bleeding in the rectum due to forced—'

'No.' This was not what he wanted to hear. 'Is she pregnant?' he asked, desperately looking for an opener.

Khurana looked startled by the abrupt change of subject. 'It's too soon to tell, but yes, she could be. I would strongly recommend an abortion.'

Juneja looked away. This wasn't what really interested him. Then it burst out of him, 'But she wanted it, I mean she said she wanted the sex. So is it really rape then?' And Juneja found himself spilling out the entire story.

Khurana looked quite pale at the end of the narrative, but his voice was steady enough. 'Nikhil, if a woman says she wants sex, it does not mean her body is prepared for it. This woman was trying to save her daughter from torture. She didn't want to have sex with those men. And believe me, if nothing else, those men *knew* it when they were battering into her.'

'So why did the daughter die and she survive?' demanded Juneja frantically, albeit a trifle inelegantly.

'From what I gather from the mother, and also your story would confirm it, the girl was a virgin. That rape is traumatic is obvious, but for a young girl who has never known sex, has never known pain in the genital or lower abdominal area, it is equally obviously much worse.'

'So,' asked Juneja clutching at straws, 'Sarbati, I mean the girl's mother, had *had* pain in her genital area?'

'I assume so.'

'Why?'

'She had experienced childbirth, hadn't she? She had had sex.'

'Childbirth is pain in the *genital* area?'

Khurana forbore to answer and looked deeply into his teacup before finally looking up. 'Nikhil, rape is a painful, traumatic assault on your body. An assault on the mind, on the spirit. Just because this woman demanded sex, as you claim she did, does not mean she was not raped. That you will have a very hard time proving this is obvious to me. And it also means that you will have to fight very hard so that she can win at least *this* battle. As far as the other two women are concerned, you have a case of murder against an unknown person or persons, but Sarbati is an eyewitness. Have you thought of that?'

Juneja nodded. He had. There had been little else to think about during the night.

'Shall we go and see the bodies together now?'

'Sure'. *Always a good idea. Seeing bodies.*

10 October 1999

Juneja woke up the next day in a daze. For the life of him he couldn't remember what he'd done the previous day. He'd gone to the morgue, spoken to Khurana, and then? Then he must have come back to his father's house. And then? He shook his head as if to clear it. There was a soft knock on the door and, without waiting for an answer, Diwan Singh walked in with a tea tray.

'It's good that you are already awake. Today is Sunday,' he said by way of greeting.

'So?' asked Juneja, yawning. His head was heavy and he considered the wisdom of a quick cup of tea and aspirin followed by a snooze.

'Today is Sunday,' said Diwan Singh again, in surprise. 'Today is the funeral service.'

Of course. That was the reason he was feeling so washed out. He had come back just before dinner yesterday. His father had been waiting for him. Khurana had told his father that an important case had come up, so he hadn't needed to offer any explanations for his absence. His father had told him about the proceedings of the funeral service. After dinner there had been no scope for awkwardness or silence. Instead, they had discussed, or gossiped, rather, about the people who had come by in the last few days. It was strange, Juneja had thought, to find himself at ease in what he now considered an alien dispensation.

He sat up and lit up in one fluid movement, despite Diwan Singh's disapproving look. It was going to be a hard day and he needed all the fortification he could lay his grubby paws on.

'Where is the newspaper?'

'Your father told me to leave it in the dining room.' Diwan Singh said. 'He said he would wait for you for breakfast,' he added with a barely disguised smile that was pure evil.

Juneja glared at him. 'Tell him I'll be down in ten minutes.'

The shower happened at the speed of light, as did the donning of the funereal garb. His father did not like waiting. It was just seven thirty when Juneja hurled himself down the stairs.

'Nikhil, what's the matter? There's no hurry. Or do you have to go off on a case again?'

'No, no, I just thought that you were ... I mean breakfast was warm, I mean ...' Juneja forced himself to stop babbling.

'I told Diwan Singh to tell you that there was no need to hurry. Today is going to be a long day. Especially in terms of emotions. We are bidding farewell to a beloved family member. I want you to know that I realize how special your grandmother was for you and that I am there for you if you need me in any way whatsoever.'

Juneja swallowed. Was he supposed to say this junk back to his father? He stuttered out some inarticulate noises, but the sight of a smirking Diwan Singh in the background made him grind to a halt.

His father must have understood his embarrassment because he turned away and walked over to the dining table.

'Your case has made it to the front page. It makes for very unpleasant reading.'

Juneja moved over to take the newspaper from his father's hand. A case had made it to the front page—just not the case that he knew about.

In the village of Arse, three women had been brutally attacked in police custody. The article neglected to mention whether the police station in question was Pankot or Miraat. At least one woman had survived. The whereabouts of the women or their bodies was currently being investigated. It was a case not unlike the Theresa Schmidt case. Sajjan Kumar, who was under investigation for that particularly barbaric crime, was said to be safe since he was under the aegis of Additional Commissioner Nikhil Juneja. Was it then a coincidence that Nikhil Juneja had been in Arse some days back? The article bore the tasteful headline: 'AN ARSE FULL OF RAPE'.

'Nikhil, you were in Arse right now, weren't you?'

'Yes, yes, I was.' He was going to have to come up with a name for his father. Calling him nothing indefinitely was getting on his nerves.

'Does this have anything to do with you?'

'Not in the way they're suggesting. I'll have to go and talk to Gupta after the service. Then everything will get cleared up.'

His father nodded his assent. 'Tell me, this young lady of yours, am I to expect her today?'

Juneja looked up from the toast he had started buttering. *Hmm, should* I *expect her today?*

'I don't know. She had to go out of town to attend a wedding.'

'And she can't make it back in time for your grandmother's funeral service? Is the wedding today?'

'I don't know.' That was a bad answer.

His father's raised eyebrows hinted that he too felt the same way.

'Well, I don't want to interfere in any way in a relationship that is clearly important to you. From my side, I would award any girl who willingly chose to spend her life with you a medal!'

Very funny. Why do parents crack such bad jokes?

On the other hand, Sanjana's chest already bears two large medals. Would she object to this particular epithet as well?

Thinking of those medals made Juneja feel that he should call her. She would definitely be all peevish and girlish because of last night but surely they could drink coffee today? It was unlikely that he would have to spend tonight at his father's house. Perhaps they could do more than drink coffee today.

Juneja attacked his breakfast with a vengeance, listening to his father babbling on about some other nonsense in the paper with only half an ear.

Sex at six, baby. Or was sex sick? Or was it just him? After all, he was willing to put up with her whingeing on and on because of it. Was he sex obsessed? Would he be willing to force a woman to have sex with him?

No, obviously not.

But that's not it, Nikhil. No, no, that is certainly not it.

So what was? When a woman said no, she meant no, right? Or was she trying to crank it up a notch?

Some of the porn he'd been surfing on the net was fairly hardcore. Not that that was bad, but the permanent eyeful of pink was somewhat boring. But the women didn't look like they were being forced. Or was doing three guys at one time force? The problem with women was that you couldn't tell. They kept their feelings, their emotions, hell, they even kept their orgasms inside. How was a man to know?

The funeral service had been organized at a hall not very far from the house. After a brief discussion as to how many cars they should take (three), the procession started off. Only the watchman was left behind in case an ignorant visitor couldn't find the way to the hall. His father's driver, his father and Juneja were the three drivers. Juneja ensured that Diwan Singh was bundled into his car. It was a short drive and Juneja needed to make the most of it. Like having a last smoke and a quick chat.

'When we go back home, you must get the third bedroom ready.'

'Who is coming to stay with us?'

'The woman, I mean, Sarbati.' She couldn't stay indefinitely at the hospital.

'The woman who said she was raped?'

Juneja drew in a breath. 'Yes.'

'She will stay with *us*?'

'You have a better idea? I can hardly send her back to Arse.'

'She can't stay with us. She is of a very low caste.'

Juneja slowed down to a crawl in a successful attempt to catch a red light.

'So? You don't have to *marry* her!'

'But she will have to eat.' Diwan Singh swallowed and continued with a certain diffidence, 'She will have to go to the bathroom.'

'So? You cook the food, give it to her and she can eat it. You don't have to feed her! She can use the servants' toilet outside, and as far as bathing is concerned, hell, she can use my bathroom. I'm not at home the entire day.'

'I should serve her food?'

There was a note in Diwan Singh's voice that made Juneja pause.

Why? Is it such *a problem?* 'What's the matter?'

His voice shaking with suppressed rage, Diwan Singh said, 'She cleans shit. She has been used by all those men, and you want me to serve her? You grandmother, your own grandmother, to whose funeral service we are going, *she* would not have been willing to even spit on this woman and you tell me to serve her?'

The venom in his voice made Juneja recoil, but Diwan Singh was relentless. 'Do you even know what you are saying to me? You drink, you smoke, you bring women over to the house, I say nothing. I say nothing to your father when he asks me. You make fun of my religious channels. You do whatever you want, I never say anything. But I will not have this. I will not. Do you hear me?'

The last was a shout.

Juneja nodded his rapid assent and this thankfully soothed Diwan Singh a little. Unable to look at Juneja, he spoke again in a mollified tone, 'Why do you want to help this woman? She said she wanted it. She is not a good woman. She is dirty. She said herself that she was not clean. Did you see her hands? Did you not smell her?'

Juneja finally found the energy to speak. 'I will make other arrangements. But if that is not possible, then you move here as long as she is there. You don't need to serve her.'

Diwan Singh looked at him with open distaste. 'You always insist on doing what you want. I am telling you, this will lead to no good.'

There was nothing he could say to that and, thankfully, there wasn't the time either.

Khurana was already there. His wife was on the podium, checking the microphone with the technicians. His father was telling the servants where to place the huge blown-up photograph of Mataji. She smiled down, permanently benevolent. A garland of flowers was placed reverently around the photograph. Yet more flowers were brought in and tastefully arranged in front of the portrait. And of course, no good Hindu service is complete without incense. How can you be spiritual unless foul-smelling smoke fills the air?

Juneja let himself be pushed around. He ferried flowers and chairs. A last-minute call had to be made to the priest who of all people had got lost and landed up at the house instead of the hall. Thank god for mobile phones! But finally, just before ten, it was all in place. Since they were immediate family, they got the worst seats of all—front row. No escape. You come first *and* you stay seated till the bitter end.

The musicians started some soulful, sombre type of music and the fat lady Started to sing.

Juneja felt himself relax physically. At last, he could think in peace. No running around, no screaming, no errands, nothing. He looked up at the beloved face smiling down at him and felt his childhood come rushing back. Songs, lullabies, all those nonsense words that constitute the private, sacred world of innocence. Had she ever been angry with him? She'd been far too clever. Her way had always been that of cajolement and love, unlike his father who was made for confrontation. She'd walked the tightrope between them.

A memory long buried sparked into life. He'd made sudden, swift friends with a servant's daughter. The way children do, today and forever, so long as you let me play with your bat. She was the sweeper's daughter. She had come from the village. He'd discovered her in the kitchen one lonely summer afternoon. He must have been seven or eight, perhaps.

It had been a golden, magical afternoon. They'd run around like little dervishes, played, screamed and fought in perfect harmony. Her name ... what was her name ... she'd had some sort of nickname; he couldn't for the life of him remember it now. But that day, that day he remembered. Not the individual details but a feeling of warmth, the recollection of perfect happiness, that for today, not forever, no, but for today I want nothing more. My cup is full.

That evening, when Mataji was putting him to bed, he announced he was going to marry Lalla. Of course, that was her name. Lalla. And Mataji had said, 'What? That sweeper's brat?' She hadn't been angry. But there had been an inflection in her voice that made Juneja shut up instinctively. He never saw the sweeper or Lalla again. He must have asked about her. At least in the beginning. But after that he had forgotten to remember.

And then, yesterday came back to him in a rush. He'd gone to Khurana and had been shown the bodies. The other old crone, shrivelled and wiped out in death. And Kasturi. Virginal and innocent Kasturi. Virginal and innocent no longer. And it was this, this, that shocked Juneja the most. Not the horrible wounds, the brutalized anus, the torn vagina. It was her face. Her face, which seemed to have developed wrinkles and aged in death.

He jerked upright in shock. His father had reached out to cover his hand. And Juneja realized that he had tears flowing down his face. For Lalla, to whom it could have happened, and for Kasturi, to whom it had. And for his grandmother, because she spat on both of them.

At the end of it, Juneja found himself being shepherded into a line at the exit. His father stood at the head of the line. As immediate family, Juneja stood next to his father. Then Khurana. That was it. A pathetic line of three men who stood with folded hands and bowed heads, attending to those taking leave of them. That was all that was left of them. People folded their hands in goodbye as they left. Some stopped to say a few words, but that was mostly to his father. Others had medical questions to ask and those were directed mostly at Khurana. Hardly anyone said anything to him. He was the recipient of the funeral-smile, a curve of the lips in greeting but lacking warmth because it was such a sad occasion. Juneja wondered if he should funeral-smile back but decided against it. Gupta was one of the few who stopped bang in front of him. Thankfully, his father was distracted.

'I'll come to the police station later,' muttered Juneja before Gupta could say anything.

Gupta nodded. 'Just a quick explanation, you know, about this newspaper article.'

The next person to stop in front of him was Sanjana. Since he was busy folding his hands and looking down modestly and sadly, the first thing he noticed was her chest. But one look at them goodies and he knew that it was She.

'Hi!' he said softly. *Was that too irreverent?*

'Hello, Nikhil.'

Perhaps. Where was his father? He seemed to have been temporarily led astray by the priest. Juneja was to wonder later if that had been prophetic.

And now? What is permissible funereal chit-chat?

Bloody hell, *he'd* lost his grandmother. Surely *she* should come up with the small talk ... or was that too much to ask for?

But she just looked really uncomfortable and finally managed to say, 'We need to talk.'

Not again! Lord save me from women who need to talk.

Why couldn't she have said, say, we need to fuck? Or in a classy way, we need to have sex? OK, it sounded distinctly asexual but he'd have said yes, sure, whenever. But talk? Alright, he could do that too. At a pinch.

'I have some errands to run for my father after this gets over. Shall we say five o'clock? Where should I pick you up?'

'I'll be at Sonia's.'

'Great, I'll see you then.'

There were no women left in the Juneja household, pondered Juneja after she'd scuttled off. Was this the right choice? After all the wrangling and coy behaviour, he hadn't even managed to introduce her to his father. Well, if he married her, he'd have to introduce her.

Rajiv and Geetu appeared.

'Really sorry, man, really sorry.' Rajiv gave him a manly thump on the back. Geetu managed a tightassed smile and a cheek rub. Intoxicated pissing was nothing compared to the death of an aged relative, and she knew it.

Juneja tried for reconciliation. 'You bad people! Where have you left the girls?' He could not for the life of him bring himself to say 'my nieces'.

Geetu thawed a bit. 'They were getting restless, so

the maids are amusing them.' She pointed in the general direction.

The maids were two young girls. They must have been around sixteen. Swantika and Dhwani looked like their children. The maids had black faces, the girls had black faces, or should that be poor faces? Were all black faces poor? Were poor faces black? The only thing awry with the picture were the expensive clothes the girls wore. Distinctly white? Certainly, identifiably rich. Or was that Geetu's effort to disguise the slum origin of her children?

Since the majority of the people had left, Juneja took the opportunity to escort them to their car. It gave him the chance to have a much-needed smoke. They left after affable farewells and more back thumping.

On the way back to the hall, Juneja stopped to have a quick word with Khurana. 'That woman who survived, you know?'

'Sarbati?'

'Yes, her. She has to stay somewhere. Or can she stay in the hospital? I mean, I could take her home but people will, you know ...' Juneja trailed off. People would think he was screwing her? He couldn't possibly betray Diwan Singh.

'I don't think anyone would believe you had designs on her, Nikhil, but I can imagine that it would be exceedingly difficult for her in a two-man household.'

Juneja nodded his head emphatically. That was it. It was her comfort he was thinking about.

'She cannot stay at the hospital indefinitely. We employ a maid and she is going on Durga Pooja leave. Let me see if Sarbati can stay in her room for a while. But Nikhil, this is a temporary arrangement, you *do* realize that?'

'Yes, yes I do. Thank you.' He couldn't manage more than that.

He decided it would be more judicious to let a servant tell his father that he was jazzing off. He'd be back for dinner as a consolation prize.

The police station was the usual noisy mess it had always been. Was it just the silence of Arse echoing in his head that made it seem so loud? The people, their fights, their aggression seemed far removed from the hellish reality he found himself trapped in.

Just about a week since he first stepped into Arse, three deaths and a funeral. It seemed like a lifetime.

Gupta had obviously just arrived and was standing in the corridor, going through the roster for the coming week.

'Ah, Nikhil, I'm glad to see you. Let's discuss this in my office.'

In the office, Gupta gestured him to a chair and started babbling, 'Nikhil, I am aware of your family situation and also that this is a particularly difficult time for you. Your grandmother was a great lady. My mother loved her like a sister. In Lahore, they were very close. I know how much you will miss her.'

Bastard, you sent me off to Arse saying I'd be back on a white horse!

Gupta meandered on about the good old Lahore days and the food in the bazaars and how they'd all hung out together, blah, blah. Gupta being a natty four-year-old. *Much you'd remember, stupid ass.*

He was interrupted by a knock on the door.

'Yes?'

'Sir, is Juneja Sir there?' It was Sinha, beaming foolishly. Joseph lurked shyly in the background.

Juneja got to his feet as the Terrible Two marched in.

'Hot coffee for you, sir,' trilled Sinha. 'We have not forgotten you, sir, even though you have forgotten us!'

Joseph had his sanctimonious look on. 'Sir, on behalf of all of us here, sir, please accept our heartiest condolences.'

Juneja solemnly shook hands with him. Was this Christian funeral etiquette?

'But you have forgotten me?' Gupta interrupted the proceedings. 'No tea for me?'

'Of course, sir, special tea is being made for you this very minute. But because we are seeing Juneja Sir after such a long time, we wanted to bring him coffee with our very own hands.'

Gupta smiled affably, while Juneja felt more removed than ever. Had he ever worked here?

'Where is Sajjan Kumar?' The Missing Link in Team Juneja.

Gupta's face tightened immediately. 'He is still under inquiry. We need to discuss that as well.' He turned to Joseph and Sinha. 'I'm sure your Juneja Sir is very happy to see you like this. After our meeting, you can tell him about all the happenings here.'

It was a clear dismissal. Joseph nodded obediently but Sinha could sniff gossip in a church.

'Sir, should I take notes or make protocol for the meeting?'

'No, Sinha, not right now. I will let you know if it's necessary. Joseph, please bring in the tea when it is ready.'

Juneja smiled sourly as Sinha plodded out his weary way. *No juice for the wicked.*

Gupta was evidently wise to Sinha's tricks and busied himself with some papers till Joseph brought in the tea. Sinha solicitously held the door open for him and waited till Joseph had accomplished this most onerous task before closing the door reluctantly.

'Like I was saying, Nikhil, I know this is a difficult time for you and your family and I don't want that you feel pressurized by work. But I am sure this newspaper article must have worried you.' He gestured at the newspaper, which had magically materialized on his table, Arse, rape, et al.

'Sir, this is a gross misrepresentation of the facts,' Juneja launched forth. He'd spent a part of the bowed-head time and the whole of the car journey coming up with a suitable version of events. In this version, Moses was not gay but a dutiful, caring, moral type of person who, at great risk to himself, had helped that one wretched surviving woman who in turn was not only the salt of the earth but also the sole witness to this most heinous of crimes. That they were the salt of the earth required no proof, other than the fact that they were poor, manual-labour type of people. That the media would also see it this way made matters simpler. That the crimes were heinous? Well, who could fail to see that. Besides Sajjan Kumar and Diwan Singh, that is.

Gupta accepted these points instinctively and without further explanation but he still looked mystified. 'But, Nikhil, why were these women attacked? How is R.P. Singh involved?'

'Because they said that the materials for the road project had not been stolen.'

'But in your report you said there had been large-scale theft!'

Juneja felt the cold spreading from his stomach. His throat dried and he had the dreadful feeling that he would lose bowel control.

With a superhuman effort, he reached for the coffee cup and took a sip. The warmth helped and the liquid eased his throat.

'The report?'

'I understand, Nikhil, you're under a lot of stress. The day of your grandmother's funeral, I came over to offer my condolences to your father. I was feeling very guilty for having sent you to this place.' Gupta looked down sadly before continuing, 'I wanted to apologize to your father, but you had managed to come for the funeral. I was very impressed by your professionalism. Despite the tragic circumstances, you had the report ready. Very impressive, my boy, very impressive!'

Impressed by his own brainlessness, Juneja tried to save face somehow. 'Sir, that report … I compiled it under a great deal of pressure. And after that I didn't really have the time to check it properly …'

'Nikhil, my boy, it is a well-written report. Very detailed, very good. In fact, I have set up a meeting next week to finalize action on the road project.'

'Sir, please let me read the report again, sir, please.' Juneja was unable to keep the sense of urgency out of his voice.

'My boy, you are on leave till the seventeenth. Take Monday off, casual leave, and spend some time with your father. You will surely accompany him to Haridwar to immerse the ashes of your beloved grandmother. We can finish these little details in your absence—'

'No! No, I won't go! No, I mean, sir, I, please, sir, let me make the presentation.'

Gupta looked startled by the vehemence and Juneja struggled hard for control.

Alarmed by the untoward emotion in Juneja's voice, Gupta said, 'Of course, my boy. I was going to delegate this to someone else. But I can understand that you want to work instead of feeling sad about your grandmother. Of course, you must make the presentation of the report. Here it is. Dussehra is on Tuesday, so shall we say Monday, the eighteenth of October?' he asked, peering at his desk calendar. 'Nine o'clock?'

'Yes, sir.'

'And Nikhil, I know that after Sajjan Kumar, police brutality is under scrutiny and you are getting a bad name by association. But this thing in Arse, we must not cover it up. If the police there is guilty, they must be punished.'

'Yes, sir, they must.'

Gupta smiled warmly at him. 'Leave Sajjan Kumar to me. You have enough to do right now. We can discuss it another time.'

'Yes, sir, we can.'

Juneja drove like a maniac to Sonia's house. She was an old friend of Sanjana's, who'd decided to opt out of the marriage market. She was now working with some dotcom NGO. She lived in East Delhi in a smelly, poky flat. Why Sanjana liked sleeping over there was a mystery to Juneja. Her own parents had a huge but shabby mansion in Lajpat Nagar. Making it through the traffic on the bridge was going to be damn near impossible. On the other hand, if he called up and said he'd be late, she'd tell him not to bother coming over.

He was just short of the Maharani Bagh crossing when his mobile rang.

He pulled over with a sigh. It was four forty. No way he could make it on time, but if he managed to inveigle her into a long conversation, he could put the blame for being late on her.

But the number on the display was unknown.

'Yes?' He took the call.

'Nikhil? Is that you? This is Muk. You know, Muk.'

'Yes, Muk, I know. What d'you want now?'

'Nikhil, can we meet? Things are very problematic here.'

'Things are pretty damn problematic here as well,' interrupted Juneja, 'thanks to your bloody boyfriend!'

'Nikhil, I need to talk to you. Moses is British. He doesn't understand India. Look, we're in Delhi and I'm trying to tell Moses that we need to leave. Please, Nikhil, please meet us this evening.'

'What d'you mean by "this evening"?'

'Well, now, any time. We're in Connaught Place. Please let's meet?'

On a Sunday?

'Connaught Place is shut on Sundays.'

Hey Nikhil, say something imbecilic.

Sorry, I can't because I already did.

'Nikhil, we're not here to shop. We're at The Imperial.'

Naturally. The Imperial. The only classy five-star hotel in town. What the hell, Sonia had only wanted to talk. Well, so did the faggots, but they came with a cold beer. Juneja would ensure they did.

'OK, I'll see you at The Imperial in a quarter of an hour.' *Nice British touch. Moses must be rubbing off on me.*

'We'll be waiting in the lobby.'

He pulled out a hot fag and lit up.

He had to stop calling *them* that! One of these days it would slip out in public and he'd look like an ass.

The Imperial was a cool place to wait and he had to figure out what he was going to say to Sanjana.

Baby, I don't feel like driving that far? Or at least not just for coffee. Or will you give me some sugar to go with it?

Fat chance of her giving sugar if you blackmail her for it.

Fair bargain, you spew, I screw?

Sure, under those circumstances, they could talk.

Juneja started the car and pulled out into the traffic. What the hell! Maybe he wouldn't call her. She hadn't been very nice this morning. It had been his grandmother's funeral service. He'd managed an invitation for her. An invite to the Juneja Funeral. There weren't many of those. Also a female one.

Nikhil, stop it. Stop it and screw her.

He wouldn't call and he wouldn't go. A last, long drag put the seal on this particularly mature decision.

From the main Ashram crossing, he went right under the flyover. Traffic was flowing fast and Juneja enjoyed the speed. The weather was perfect. He didn't need the AC, and the sun, although warm, had lost its hateful sting.

The Purana Qila on Mathura Road looked magnificent. The conveniently located red traffic light enabled him to admire the red sandstone and slate bathed in the pinky gold of the setting sun. Delhi had always been a city for royalty. Even though the British hadn't originally wanted Delhi as their capital, in the end they had settled here. They'd had to. Because Delhi was headquarters. Historical headquarters.

Next to the fort (or was it *in* the fort?) was the Delhi Zoo, a place where he'd spent many wintery Sundays of his childhood. His father had been his proud escort, and on several memorable occasions, Khurana. It was magnificent. And today it was just a zoo.

That made sense: forts and monkeys, the same thing. Take one portion royal accommodation, let it become old and crumbly. Then throw in some monkeys and then … and then? Then it becomes a historical location, a backdrop. You could stage theatrical productions there. Actors monkeying around on a stage, playing roles. That was how it worked. That was Delhi—royal, majestic, noble. The Mughals had done it and the British had perfected it—The Art of Monkeying Around. Pretend you're all benevolent and caring, interested in development and equitable distribution of wealth. After all, only those who had oodles of money could distribute it, right?

The fags were sitting in the lobby. Anyone could tell they were gay—they were holding hands. *Sick bastards.*

'So, where's the fire? Big Daddy's here to help the little boys!'

'Nikhil, don't talk like that,' answered Muk, getting to his feet. Moses looked unperturbed by his brusqueness.

'Look, your friend, I'm sorry, your boyfriend, your life partner, your meaningful other half has put a shitload of trouble on my plate. I have to handle it on my own. The two of you are evidently making holiday plans and need my help in making your bookings. Somehow I'm not too thrilled. I mean, did I mention my grandmother died? Does it cross your mind that I could actually be doing stuff?' *When did I become so American?*

Juneja turned to Muk. Moses was ignoring him in any case. 'You're Indian, Muk, or have you forgotten your culture to such an extent that you don't even realize that today was the chauttha?'

Moses looked askance.

'Funeral service, a mourning ceremony,' supplied Muk before turning back to Juneja. 'I'm sorry, I didn't know. How could I?'

'Your boyfriend could have told you! He dragged me out. I had to leave my father alone and dash off to the back of bloody beyond to save his ass!' shot off Juneja.

Milk it, man, milk it! No more female funerals coming up in a hurry.

Muk raised his hands in supplication. 'OK, Nikhil, I'm sorry, I'm really sorry. Look, let's go up to our room and—'

'You have a room here?' *They must be loaded.*

'We have to sleep somewhere, or are you offering your apartment?' The sardonic query was from Moses who was the only one still sitting.

Juneja ignored this silliness. 'No, I am not willing to go up to your room with you.'

'Scared to turn your back on us? You're not our type. We prefer our gang rapes young and perky!'

'Like all the other men in Arse? Sure you weren't a part of the crowd? After all, back-door entries are your specialty, aren't they?' shot back Juneja.

'You asshole!'

'You see those everywhere. That must be a real obsession with you. You should see a therapist.'

Moses got to his feet slowly.

'Stop it, Mo, just stop it. We are not going to have a slanging match or a physical fight. Nikhil, please, we need to talk.'

'So, talk!'

'Here in the lobby?'

'I am not going to your bedroom!'

'OK, shall we go to 1911? Have a drink? Nikhil, please, we really need your help!'

Juneja nodded his assent. He'd been hoping for the Spice Route but 1911 wasn't too shabby either.

Nobody spoke till the waiter had left with the order. Two beers and a fresh lime soda.

'So, why d'you need my help again?' asked Juneja, allowing the condescension to lovingly seep through.

'You know, Nikhil, I don't get it.' Moses looked flabbergasted. 'We haven't committed any crime! We're the good people here. I got that woman to justice. We're being threatened by Raghu, or at least by his thugs, and you're acting as if you're doing us a favour! You're the bloody police!'

Juneja looked at him.

'Brought the woman to justice? Since when does she need justice? She'd probably have been better off dead! Now the entire road project is in jeopardy, her village continues to be stranded till this entire mess is over, and I have a load of grief! And you say to me you haven't committed a crime?'

'*Since when does she need justice?*' Moses looked like he was going to faint. 'Nikhil, listen to yourself. She's poor and that's what's killing you, isn't it? Having to help someone who is poor?'

'Stop it, Mo.' Muk waved aside his partner's vituperations with an airy gesture. 'Nikhil, the point is, our position in Miraat–Pankot is very precarious. Although nothing has happened as yet, Raghu seems to suspect that we had a hand in this affair. He dropped by a couple of days ago and asked some weird questions.'

'Well, I can change that for you,' offered Juneja helpfully. 'Raghu won't need to ask you any questions any more. He'll be able to read the answers in the newspaper. I've just spoken to my boss and thanks to him and your boss here …' Juneja nodded at Moses, '… we are cracking down on police brutality. This means that the truth will come out or we can nail whichever poor slobs Raghu has lined up for us. Either way, Moses and the little role he essayed in his quest for justice will not go unnoticed.'

Muk shook his head. 'What are we going to do? If we ask for police protection, will we get it?'

'Police protection? For a couple of fags?'

Moses slammed a hand on the table, making a few other people in the bar turn around, but his voice when he spoke to Muk was barely a whisper, 'How can you put up with this?'

Muk smiled at him. 'This is the way it is, Mo. What did you expect? I didn't belong in your country as a black and I don't belong here as a gay man. Neither do you. Neither did that woman you insisted on rescuing. She was supposed to clean toilets and keep her mouth shut. You insisted on giving her hot water and clothes and trying to get her to sit at the table with us, and look where it's landed us! Packing up and leaving everything all over again. So stop being mad at him. At least he's being honest!'

Partly mollified by Muk's acknowledgement of his honesty, Juneja allowed himself to tell them the truth. Or at least the truth as he saw it. In Arse or Pankot or Miraat, the police could do nothing to help them. If Raghu wanted them out, out they would be. As far as Delhi was concerned, they could try setting up home and hearth, but earning a living was a different ballgame and the cost of living was definitely higher than in Arse.

The conversation went on and on in circles. Muk and Moses took turns being desperate or defiant. By nine o'clock, Juneja had had enough and got up to leave. By this time they were on more or less friendly terms. The level of alcohol in their blood probably had something to do with it—Muk had joined them during a desperate phase.

The final decision had been to (a) almost 90 per cent leave Miraat or (b) almost 95 per cent go to Delhi or London, which was the same thing. Or not, considering immigration laws in the UK regarding same-sex partnerships (or LGBT as Moses kept calling it) were problematic. Juneja asked Moses if LGBT meant *Lag Gayi Beta Teri* but Muk shut him up with a look and told Moses it was untranslatable rubbish.

In a fit of bonhomie or probably a lack of anything better to do, they walked Juneja to the car park.

'Isn't it funny, Nikhil?' asked Moses suddenly, 'all this money, this flamboyance really, on display here? I mean Delhi isn't very far from Miraat, but it's like another planet, another world, isn't it?'

'That's true of London and Delhi too!' asserted Juneja, letting slip a discreet burp. All that beer had made him distinctly gassy.

'Well, Delhi and London aren't the same country and are about thousands of kilometres apart so, no, it's not at all the same thing. But what I'm saying is that there's such fear associated with Arse and what's happened there.'

'Well, not everyone likes gang rape and murder, you know. And, Moses, my god, what is there *not* to be scared about? If someone gets murdered in your neighbourhood, don't you think it could happen to you? Aren't you scared?'

'That's not it, Nikhil.'

'No,' broke in Muk, 'he's right, Nikhil, that's not it. It's not that people are scared of gang rape. That's normal in Delhi. People get raped and killed every day. But they don't like seeing who it has happened to.'

Moses nodded.

Oh joyous gay epiphany!

'You've got it. They don't like the idea of this woman being alive. Of her being able to say what happened to her. I saw the look on the faces of those other two policemen, Nikhil. They weren't sorry for her but they were outraged that she dared say it.'

And my face? What did I betray?

Moses went on, 'You're always poker-faced, but they were disgusted by her and were afraid of her. It was as if everyone's best kept secret was being aired.'

'OK boys, enough theatricals. It's late and all good children must be in bed.' He stuck out a hand for Moses to shake but Moses gave a rueful smile, pushed the hand away and pulled him into a very careful, non-threatening embrace. Despite his initial shock, Juneja realized that Moses was being extremely careful—his pelvis was pulled away and only their shoulders, arms and faces came into the lightest, gentlest contact.

'Thanks, Nikhil, I know it hasn't been easy for you. And I also understand that we imposed extra stress on you at the time of your grandmother's death. I don't know if we'll be meeting again in the near future but I'm going to try and stay in touch, OK?'

Touched, Juneja nodded his assent. There wasn't much that topped gay chatter in any case.

The hug with Muk was silent and after a last soothing twitch of his eyebrows, Juneja climbed into the car and exited The Imperial.

He discovered almost immediately that he had only two cigarettes left and drove into the Inner Circle to find an open fag shop.

It had been inaccurate to say that it was late. It just seemed that way in CP. It was always a little eerie at night. During the day it was all hustle bustle. But at night, although there were pockets of activity in front of stand-alone restaurants, it was as if a pall had been cast over the place. Beggars were settling in for the night. After a day of pleading and wheedling, they sank down on garbage heaps, ready to chase the dragon. The parking lots, filled to capacity in the day, lay open and empty to the dusty skies. A large motorcycle boomed past, startling him out of his reverie. It also drew his attention to the fag shack on the pavement.

He pulled over and bought the cigarettes and on a whim decided to drink a Coke to accompany his hot fag. The glimmering rope hanging from the side of the shop gave him a light and he parked his backside on the side of the car and took a long, cold swig from the bottle.

Across the road, a family lay sleeping on the pavement. In lieu of a mattress, they had plastic bags. The sound of cars and traffic or the conversation of the passers-by didn't seem to disturb them.

And that is what scares me. Nothing disturbs them. Nothing hurts them. They want nothing because they have so little that they have never learnt to want. They are naked in their poverty and I am scared because under all this I could also be naked. They could make me naked.

Maybe it was just the ghostly atmosphere. Maybe it was the truth.

11 October 1999

Juneja woke up the next morning to a silent apartment. Diwan Singh was still in his father's house. Perhaps he would go later and tell him that other arrangements had been made for Sarbati.

He heaved himself out of bed, unused to such a lonely morning. The kitchen, always an unknown area, seemed to mock his incompetence and it seemed fitting to drop the entire breakfast thing rather than labouring at a farce.

It was eight o'clock and Juneja decided, in a fit not entirely inspired by his growling stomach, that he could ask Rajiv out for breakfast. Geetu couldn't possibly protest since it would, by its very nature, have to be a meeting without alcohol. Monday was Rajiv's half-day and he often went in late to work. So they had a good chance of meeting. Maybe he could discuss the entire Sanjana thing with him. Maybe even the Arse thing.

The good thing was he could call Rajiv directly on his mobile. That way they could circumnavigate the entire Geetu problem. Maybe even tell a small, white lie. Something about unexpected work …

'Hi! Rajiv? It's me, Nikhil!'

'Hi, Nikhil.' The usually cheerful voice sounded curiously flat.

'What's up, man? Don't tell me I've woken you up?'

'No, Nikhil, not at all. With the girls, you know, we've all become early risers. I mean, Geetu always got up early. But I do too now.'

Right. The poor girls. That was something you'd forgotten. The budding father wouldn't jazz off for breakfast now, would he?

'I wanted to ask you if you wanted to grab a bite.' Juneja heard the stupidity of the request in the utterance of it. It was totally lame.

'A bite? You mean dinner?' Rajiv sounded shocked. What was happening?

'No, I actually meant breakfast,' responded Juneja.

'Now?' Rajiv sounded even more thunderstruck. 'I was just reading the newspaper …' His voice trailed off.

'Well, you know Diwan Singh's still at my dad's place,' said Juneja, aware he had to offer some reason for the invitation, 'and I thought, you know, we haven't met for some time and, you know, you have the girls in the evening …' *Shut up, Nikhil, shut up!*

As if suddenly pulling himself together, Rajiv said, 'Nikhil, I'll come over in an hour, OK?'

Nonplussed by the turnabout, Juneja said, 'Great! I'll be downstairs, waiting.'

Shat, showered and shaved, Juneja went down, a newspaper and a cigarette in hand. He had made it into the papers. Or rather, yet another article about Arse had.

This one claimed that to prevent details of the road scam breaking out, the police had beaten up poor villagers and also raped a few chicks while they were at it. Unlike the other report, this one claimed the direct involvement of one Nikhil Juneja. The article then prattled on and on about the Bhagalpur blindings, custodial deaths and rapes, and ended with an ode to Sajjan Kumar, brutalizer and rapist par excellence.

Juneja started laughing about the inconsistencies in the article until he realized that Rajiv had arrived, looking rather grim.

'Hey buddy, what's up?'

'If you can laugh while you're reading that, Nikhil, I really don't know what to say to you!'

'Rajiv, OK, I'll be serious but you know this article is crap! It's just the usual nonsense that the media comes up with to indulge in some cop bashing!'

'Policemen who rape innocent women deserve to be bashed,' answered Rajiv with a prim twitch of his lips.

'OK, OK, we'll bash those guys. But it wasn't a policeman who raped these women. It was the villagers who did it!'

'Look, Nikhil, I would have said this on the phone but since you're my oldest friend I wanted to say it in person.'

I'm your oldest friend, not your best *friend? You wanted to see me bleed in person, rather than take in the indignity on the phone?*

Rajiv's message was short and sweet. 'You don't realize, Nikhil, because you never want to take responsibilities. We have two girls now. And we thought you would be like an uncle to them. Instead, the newspapers are full of your involvement in yet another rape case!'

'Rajiv, what the hell does that mean? I'm not permanently involved in rape cases!'

'So you say, but this is the second this month, Nikhil, and the month isn't over. We don't want to be associated with this kind of heinous crime!'

Juneja looked at his shoes, stunned that Rajiv could use a word like *heinous* in normal conversation.

'So, what was the first case?'

'Nikhil, are you raping so many women that you don't even remember Theresa Schmidt?' Rajiv was shouting.

'Screw you, Rajiv. And thanks for the breakfast.'

Juneja turned to storm out only to realize that he was in his own apartment. No sweat. He marched to his car, ready to storm.

Cruising to nowhere in the car, Juneja wondered whether he should pick up Diwan Singh. The apartment had been distinctly bachelor hostile this morning. But if Diwan Singh was going to go all casteist and funny, there was little joy to be had from his company.

Maybe it's time to grow up, Nikhil. Men live alone in America. In Europe.

He could cook and clean. Well, he could definitely go home and see what was in the fridge and then get himself a load of kebabs and beer. Some home delivery menus. Maybe some frozen food of some sort. Bastard Diwan Singh would come back crawling.

And if he didn't, well, living in Juneja's father's house would screw his happiness—no cable, no devotional channels. And in the meantime, Juneja could invest some valuable time checking out some top-grade porn. What's not to be happy about? Sod Rajiv and Diwan Singh—bloody servant class getting above itself.

All told, things were going to work out. Even if he had submitted a cooked-up report, Juneja figured, damage control was possible. With the entire world going on and on about how impossible it was for Rt Hon. Raghu to have raped those women, the same logic could apply to him, Nikhil Juneja!

He too had found it impossible to believe that Raghu could be capable of a scam. He had been so blinded, so dazzled, so impressed by Raghu that he had stupidly, naively, blindly made that report. Only after the women had been raped had he realized what the situation actually was.

As public perception goes or, he mused, could be made to go, here was a policeman who selflessly, with nary a thought for himself or his dead granny, had road-dashed around the place, and gathered information and safeguarded the solitary eyewitness to this terrible, terrible crime against humanity in general and womankind in particular.

It was a bit far-fetched, but Juneja knew he could get away with it. He had good reason to believe so.

Gupta would want to back him up. The story showed the police in great light. They were an impressionable, youthful but intrinsically honest police force. Moreover, the police was woman-friendly. That was always good. At this point it was especially good, considering the entire Sajjan Kumar investigations. In fact, this was the one aspect that gave Juneja's conscience a teeny-weeny twinge—SK's head could land up on the chopping block if the powers that be decided to make a precedent of the case.

The media would like it too. It gave them the opportunity to gently mock the police and at the same time pat themselves on the back for having uncovered a crime. Watchdogs of society and all that. *Bunch of fucking mongrels.*

And finally, no money had changed hands. Raghu had offered the money and he'd theoretically accepted it but the actual transaction had not happened. Sure, they'd shaken on it and thumped backs and traded gentlemanly vows, but there's many a sticky drip betwixt cup and lip. And a sherbety one it had been. But all things said and done, the greenbacks were not in his possession. Sure, Raghu could claim he'd bribed Nikhil Juneja but how could he prove it? Swiss bank accounts, hawala schemes, anonymous land holdings—nothing, nada.

And once Nikhil Juneja, Saviour of the Female Race, had prevailed, Raghu would be sucking eggs in jail. Rajiv and Geetu would pine for him. They'd wish they'd stuck by him because he'd be a hero. A hero for all women.

Feeling slightly light-headed, Juneja cast a scornful look at the crossing and the vendor boy offering him the Ikea catalogue, stuck a cigarette at a jaunty angle in his mouth and drove off with a slight squeak of the tyres. Discreet and classy. It showed scorn but also, mostly, that he didn't care.

Since he was driving past the Green Park market, Juneja decided to put his plan into action without further ado.

Green Chick Chop yielded five kilos of assorted kebabs.

The bloody booze shop was closed since it was only ten o'clock in the morning and all booze shops opened only at noon. But Juneja knew the fool who ran it and had no compunctions about calling him. Bastard lived in some garage not too far. He was there in ten minutes, oily smile and hair in place.

'Good morning, sir! Why did you take the trouble? Just one call and Diwan Singh could have picked it up! For special customers ...' He gave Juneja a meaningful smile. '... I will be offering free home delivery soon.'

Juneja smiled back condescendingly.

'And what mood is sir in today?'

Lousy, so don't push it. 'I'll take some beer.'

'Sir, top-quality whisky has come in yesterday, top quality.'

Juneja shook his head. Indian whisky was slop.

'Just beer is fine.'

'Kingfisher, Foster's?'

'Kalyani Black?' asked Juneja hopefully.

'Sir, you are very traditional, very traditional! No, sir, today only Kingfisher and Foster's sell. If I get Kalyani Black, nobody buys. Who wants old-fashioned beer? Only modern!'

'Well, if you get it again, call me and I'll take it. Now just give me three cartons of Kingfisher.'

'Sir, please bring the car behind the shop. I will bring it to the car. Sir, you see, the shop hasn't opened yet, so we will have to take backside!'

Sure. Aren't we all taking it?

He was almost at the police station when he realized that he was actually on leave and had no reason being there. But what the hell! It wasn't as if he was expected elsewhere and he could do with a chinwag with his cronies.

He decided to park the car a little away from the police station rather than in the designated parking. With the car full of kebabs and clinking bottles, it could be embarrassing if someone decided to escort him back to the car.

He would enter the police station from the front like any common citizen and then sneak up on that lazy bastard Sinha for a cup of tea and some cosy gossip. Maybe something to eat with that. The breakfast with Rajiv had only been a feast of words.

He lit up and started walking the hundred-odd metres to the station. Was he crazy or was the entrance festooned with placards and posters? He was already in their midst when he remembered Theresa Schmidt and her posthumous quest for justice.

It was a crowd that consisted almost entirely of women. But there were men present. The pyjama-kurta variety or the earnest, dipped in dust and shit, torn jeans kind.

Must be the riff-raff from the nearby university. It had always been radical left, thought Juneja. *Probably their idea of a little outing. Bastards should be studying instead of wasting the taxpayers' money like this.*

He moved in, trying to make himself inconspicuous. A kind of photo exhibition had been set up. Hoping that he could present everyone with a view of the back of his not identifiable head, Juneja moved forward to take a look. It was Theresa Schmidt, her life and times. Born in Hannover, studied some bloody social work and pedagogy in Heidelberg, blah, blah, and copped it in Delhi.

Yes, we know. But we didn't know that there would be pictures of a torn and battered body on display now, did we? What was this? A demonstration against police brutality or a porn exhibition? Perhaps I should arrest them.

Unwilling to gape but unable to stop, Juneja found himself rooted to the spot, staring alternately at his feet and at the pictures.

'Terrible, aren't they?'

It was a young girl. Probably one of the students.

'Shocking,' he managed.

'She was devastated. You know she was a virgin?'

'I beg your pardon?' Juneja was thunderstruck.

'She was very religious. Jehovah's Witness. That's why she committed suicide. Because she was no longer pure.'

'You seem to have known her rather well.'

'I'm sorry, I haven't introduced myself, I'm Smriti Advani. I work with an NGO for underprivileged children. Theresa used to do volunteer work with us. She was very strong on social commitment and had a strong social conscience.'

'Hi, I'm Nikhil, Nikhil Jain. I work, I mean, I have a business. Actually, we have been having some problems in the factory and I needed to file an FIR for the insurance claim. And then I saw your, umm, exhibition, so I looked in, I mean, I'd already read about the case and so I came in.' He'd pulled it off rather well. Maybe he could try for a job with RAW. Change his name permanently to Nikhil Jain and then he might even get to screw her.

Smriti Advani evidently took the entire thing terribly seriously. On closer inspection, he realized that she was older than he'd thought originally. It must be the lack of make-up. And perhaps she was quite hot for him? She'd stepped forward, hadn't she?

'You know, not very many men support our cause. So when you came in I thought I'd, you know, check whether you're a reporter or something. There are even some men who come in to see the pictures of a naked woman. A naked, dead woman is *porn* for them. It turns them *on*, can you beat that?'

'Well, I'm genuinely interested. Cigarette?' asked Juneja, anxious to change the subject.

'Thanks, but I have my own.' And she had the temerity to pull out a packet of Dunhill.

Rich bitch. Or maybe she is trying to impress me. 'So you were saying, she was a virgin?' *Let's get back to the main issue.*

'I think so, I mean she definitely said she didn't believe in premarital sex, you know. And it's such a tragedy because the fucking police is trying to make out that she was some slutty, floozy, foreigner ...' She punctuated each word with airy inverted commas. '... So stereotypical, so male.'

'So invasive,' agreed Juneja, trying to remember some of Sanjana's diatribe.

She gave him a startled look before she slowly nodded, 'Yes, it's a horrible invasion of her space.'

Space! That's right, it invaded her personal space because the personal is the historical? That can't be right, so don't say it. 'So, so, what's the status now?'

'Well, we're trying to put as much pressure on the police as possible so that an independent inquiry can be set up. We're determined to nail this bastard Sajjan Kumar.'

Right. Juneja nodded, sure he could understand that.

'As well as some kind of reprimand for his superior, Juneja.'

Really? 'Is he responsible?'

'Well, not directly. But, you know, he lets others do the dirty work for him. He's kept this Sajjan Kumar as his private goon and the payback is that he gets to rape women!'

Startled by this understanding of his affairs, Juneja tried desperately to change the subject. 'So, what about Theresa Schmidt's family?'

'They've just gone back last week. They were totally devastated.'

Juneja gave more understanding nods.

'I mean, just look at her.'

Juneja gave the photograph a sidelong glance. It showed Theresa Schmidt's body covered till the neck with a sheet. OK, he could look at that.

'She finally looks at peace, doesn't she? All the pain, the agony wiped out? She told me, she begged and pleaded with him, but he wouldn't stop. She said it was agonizing pain.' Smriti stopped to compose her trembling voice. 'I'm sorry, I try and tell as many people as I can, so that we can mobilize more people. But it's so hard to talk about.'

Juneja nodded. There wasn't much to say.

At one end of the tent was a donation box. He put some money in and left for home. There didn't seem to be any point in going into the police station after all.

Juneja returned home staggering under the weight of his custom. It was a sad thought that he had no one to share the bounty with. Calling over acquaintances when he was on leave on compassionate grounds due to his granny's death and when he was in the newspapers for rape and death just didn't seem appropriate. Rajiv had behaved like an idiot, which could be either his wife finally emerging as the alien predator in his body, or fatherhood. Sanjana, well, as Bachchan said in *Sholay*, would probably just remain yet another unfinished story. What the fuck! There wasn't any shortage of those in his life. And Smriti? Well, maybe another time …

He wondered if he should call Muk and Moses over. At least there was a remote chance that they would cook. Perhaps Muk would clean. They could have Diwan Singh's room. Would they mind? Would they know it was a servant's room? Muk would. The Indian nose was quick to sniff out social iniquities. Moses being a foreigner wouldn't care. Maybe he'd even like it. Levelling out the injustices and all that. He'd probably say that a room where the servant stays is a room where the servant stays; it's not the 'servant's room'. Even though it was.

Plus, they could save money. After all The Imperial didn't come cheap. On the other hand, he might be compromising witnesses and all that nonsense.

So, what should he do? Maybe the M&Ms would want to meet up for a drink? Moses had said he wanted to stay in touch.

Juneja called up The Imperial but no one had checked in under the name of Schuwelbaum. Perhaps they'd checked in under Muk's name, which he didn't know.

Did he know the room number? No, since he'd refused to go up.

So?

So, thank you for your help, which was nonexistent, and bye-bye.

He put away the kebabs, carefully keeping a packet out for the evening. A carton of beer went into the chiller tray.

What should he do now? Porn at noon? Nah, didn't feel like it. Even though he should probably start practising. Sanjana wasn't likely to feature in the future.

He flopped down on a yellow cushion and put on the TV. *Santa Barbara* followed by *The Bold and the Beautiful.* Old Hindi film with Vinod Mehra. News. Rerun of some cricket match—New Zealand vs Zimbabwe. Ye gads, he wouldn't have wanted to watch that *live.*

What did people watch on TV?

He pottered around the apartment, but given that there were only the three and a half rooms, that didn't take up much time.

Back to TV. For lack of anything better to see, he started checking out the devotional channels.

The cable guy responsible for the selection was clearly of the opinion that his main customer base was Hindu. He received seven Hindu religious channels to one Muslim one. The Muslim one was explaining the correct way to wash, i.e., the Quranic wash method. Juneja watched, temporarily entranced by the thought that there were people who wished to wash Quranically. There were separate guidelines for female washing. Unfortunately, his Urdu wasn't up to the mark and it soon became boring. Besides, Quranic washing was fun only when you could share it with someone.

The Hindu channels seemed to be devotional MTV. Lots of singing and dancing. None of it in the tiny clothes he was so fond of and therefore ultimately uninteresting.

Back to New Zealand–Zimbabwe?

C'mon, Nikhil get a life, do something!

What?

Anything.

What?

Read a book? That's something people can do alone.

OK, let's have a look at the bookshelf.

The official bookshelf, as opposed to the one at the bottom of his cupboard, had been instated by Sanjana. It rounded off his personality, she'd said; gave it depth. Juneja privately thought it offset the gaudy colour scheme she'd come up with. The books at least looked sombre. He'd never glanced at the titles.

The top shelf was leather bound. Charles Dickens, Jane Austen and Thomas Hardy. Gave him quite a hard-on.

The second shelf was also hardbound, but these were books no one in their right mind would ever want to buy—condensed *Readers' Digest* versions of books. Since *Readers' Digest* had done the condensing, there was no sex or violence of any kind, discovered Juneja rapidly. People didn't even procreate.

He returned to the third and final shelf, which turned out to be the self-help section. There were books on how to make friends, better colleagues and bookshelves. There was also a guide to home decoration.

Why was there no guide on how to buy books? Or on how to keep a girlfriend? How to have sex on a regular basis?

The sheer boredom of it all was making his eyes droop. *What the hell!* There was nothing to do in any case and he gave in to the whim. Pulling up his legs on to the sofa, he let himself fall asleep.

An aching arm trapped under the weight of his body forced him to wake up a few hours later. He felt unrefreshed and disoriented after his nap. More so when he realized that it was only two o'clock in the afternoon and he was still alone.

It was an agonizing day. Despairing, Juneja finally decided to lie in bed and consider the ceiling. It didn't tell him much.

When the telephone eventually rang at five o'clock in the evening, he almost wept with gratitude.

'Hello?'

'Nikhil, your father said you were back in your own apartment.'

It was Gupta.

'Good evening, sir!'

'Yes, good evening, Nikhil! Nikhil, I am sorry but we are going to have to take a difficult decision. I can understand that you have put in a lot of work on this road scam project and you want to present the report but I'm afraid I cannot wait till Monday.'

Juneja felt his knees weaken with relief. Gupta was going to cut short his leave. He would have an excuse to go back to work.

'Nikhil, I have decided to reallot the case to someone else because I don't want to cut short your leave at such a tragic time—'

'No, sir! Please, sir, please don't do that, sir! Please, sir!' *Lord, is there no end to this torture?*

'Nikhil, my boy, I understand but I am under a lot of pressure. This fellow, Raghavendra Pratap Singh, has a lot of political clout and the villagers in this wretched place have surrounded the local police station and are demanding justice. Some policeman there has already admitted to the crime. Or at least this Raghavendra Pratap Singh says he has. He also says that the police is trying to frame him. Meanwhile, the police station where the FIR was filed in this rape case is claiming a different story. Some police fellow there, some Varma-Sharma, has already given an interview to the press. Stupid bastard. Did you see it on Star?'

No, I was watching the ceiling channel. 'Why would the police want to frame Raghu, I mean, Raghavendra Pratap Singh?'

'To escape the rape charge. Also he says ...' Here, Gupta's voice changed into forced neutrality. 'He says that you wanted a bribe for the road report. And that you are trying to pin the rape on his poor villagers as revenge.'

'But I made a report clearing him of any wrongdoing!'

'And you wanted a bribe for that. But since a clean report was his due, he didn't see why you should get money to write it!'

Game, Set and Match.

The bastard had really knotted up every loose end. Except for Sarbati. Raghavendra Pratap Singh must be shitting bricks.

'Sir, please don't take the case away from me. Please, sir, I will be happy to cut my leave short. The name of our department cannot be dishonoured this way! I'll be back at work tomorrow!'

'Nikhil, my boy!' Gupta was touched beyond belief.

Juneja smiled smugly. The dishonour bit was a classic touch. Or should he have gone for besmirched? Gupta may not have understood. The obvious was better.

'But, Nikhil, tomorrow—'

'Sir, please, this is an order. I will be back tomorrow!' Another smooth piece of work.

'My boy, I don't know what to say. If we had more officers like you, the Delhi Police Force would be ...' Gupta stopped again. Just as well. Saying anything would mean confessing that the Delhi Police was lolling around in the gutter right now.

'Nikhil, I am looking at my schedule right now and, unfortunately, tomorrow I have a court hearing and on Wednesday there's an interdepartmental inquiry into Sajjan Kumar's alleged involvement in the Theresa Schmidt case. I tell you, Nikhil, this is becoming very uncomfortable. I cannot postpone any of these. Also, my secretary will need to organize your presentation. So shall we say Thursday? Fourteenth October? Ten o'clock? Sharp?

'Yes, sir.' Juneja allowed for a meaningful pause before continuing with a controlled wobble, 'Sir, it is my honour that you are trusting me. Thank you, sir. And I know my grandmother would also thank you.'

Game, Set, Match, Championship.

It was as if a huge weight had been lifted from his shoulders. Who knew a human voice could bring about such relief? And that too Gupta's creaky, croaky tenor. He should celebrate. He *would* celebrate. He would get out of this stupid, silly apartment and get himself a good dinner and by the time he came home, the beer would be cold. Or he could just go for a long drive. Check out the city. Maybe even go shopping. It was only five thirty in the evening. He could go to South Ex. and get himself some shoes. Some cool threads. *Stop calling them threads, Nikhil—the eighties are over.*

Charged with a new reason to live, Juneja had a quick shower. The cool water made him tingle and he could feel his muscles relax slowly. Who'd have thought time off could be so stressful?

He pulled on an old, faded pair of jeans and a relatively new but soft T-shirt. Comfort clothing. His soul still felt bruised.

He'd almost left the apartment when the mobile rang again.

It was Sanjana.

He saw the name on the display. *What the hell.* He'd have to get this sorted out, sooner or later.

'Hi, Sanjana!'

'Nikhil, very kind of you to answer the call after you saw my name.'

'I couldn't find the phone. That's what caused the delay. I didn't have the time to look, although you're right, that could've put me off.' *Real smooth, Nicky boy.*

'Look, Nikhil, I haven't called to snipe with you.'

No?

'I called Rajiv today to ask him if he knew what the matter was and he told me about your reaction.'

She made it sound like animal porn.

'So? I can tell Rajiv what I think!'

'Nikhil, have you seen the news? I don't think you know what you're doing! Look, I'm in South Ex. right now. I'll come over and we can talk.'

'Sanjana, you do what you want. I have another call coming through and I know what I'm doing.'

This time round, he did take the call without checking the ID of the caller. 'Hello?'

'Nikhil, have you seen the news?'

There was no mistaking *that* voice. The progenitor.

'No, I've been busy today.'

'Well, I suggest you watch the news at six o'clock. I assume there will be a repeat show at that time. Nikhil, I hope you realize what you have gotten into. I have spoken to Peshi Khurana and he has absolved you of any wrongdoing but I am startled and saddened by the nature of your work.'

Who speaks like this?

Juneja could feel the newly won euphoria degenerating into the much more familiar ball cringe. He was saddened but not very startled.

'Well, I'll watch the news at six and get back to you.'

'Nikhil, one more thing, where is your young lady at this time?'

Clearly, South Ex. was not the appropriate answer.

'How d'you mean?'

'Is she by your side?'

'I don't know.' But since nothing ventured, nothing gained, Juneja went in for the jugular. 'Are you?'

The silence was not the answer he was expecting. And that was startling.

A little dry in the throat, he asked again, 'Are you?'

'Since I don't know which side you are on, Nikhil, I don't know.'

Right. So much for thick and thin. 'OK, so, I'll watch the news and let you know.'

'I'll be looking forward to it.'

Excellent.

That put paid to the shopping and the shopaholic. Juneja put some seekhs into the microwave and pulled out a bottle of beer. It was evening and he hadn't eaten the entire day and why care, or rather, who cares what anybody thinks!

The news started just as he sat back. Kebab platter on the side table, beer glass to his lips.

It was breaking news. *He* was breaking news.

'It was a shocking incident that scandalized Delhi and sent shock waves resounding through the capital. Theresa Schmidt, a young German social worker, was brutally raped at a police station.'

Cut to Theresa Schmidt frolicking with children.

Bitch didn't look young. She had haunches like a stud bull.

'She came here to work with poor, impoverished children.'

No, she didn't. She came to work with some chicks who'd also been screaming rape or some such crap. She was only volunteering with Smriti's outfit. At least get your facts right.

Cut to calendar.

'On the fourteenth of September, Theresa Schmidt went to the Basantpur police station in posh South Delhi to file an FIR for petty pilferage happening at her workplace.'

Was it one of the raped chicks who'd been stealing, or one of your impoverished children?

Cut to an old photograph of the police station with, ye gads, his own mug grinning. 'What happened there is a matter of horror and shame. Constable Sajjan Kumar, who was allegedly the policeman on duty that evening, brutally raped her.'

Cut to picture of Kasturi.

No, it was Theresa Schmidt. The report was about her.

It wasn't Kasturi. Juneja shook his head as if to clear it—he was seeing dead women everywhere.

But then they did cut to pictures of Kasturi and the crone. Dharmi. Her name was Dharmi—the righteous one. Not the photographs of their battered bodies but of their terribly dead faces.

They showed Sajjan Kumar. It was his file photograph. They showed Nikhil Juneja. He was grinning at some function. They showed Arse—green and lush.

The sound of a neighbour's bell ringing suddenly reminded him that he'd given Sanjana carte blanche to come over. The thought of entering into yet another have-you-thought-of-the-consequences-of-your-actions conversation revolted him.

Never mind the beer, Nikhil, just hit the road.

Logic demanded that if Sanjana had been in South Ex., she could no longer be there. She could, of course, have spies lurking in the corners. But then he could always say that he'd misunderstood. That she'd told him to meet her there. Besides, who cared about her fucking spies? The point was to *not* meet her.

He made it to the Uphaar crossing at a remarkable speed only to be caught in a massive jam at AIIMS, which didn't bother him any. He had time to spare. The jam was due to the massive construction going on at the crossing. Major plans for a looping flyover there.

Maybe it too was a flyover scam. Maybe it wasn't. Maybe, at the end of it, it would give shelter to homeless people, like all flyovers did. Maybe it would be a perfectly landscaped jewel of the city. Maybe it would become an open-air brothel instead. That would be something. In the heart of the city, mad, wild sex. Perhaps not a brothel but a place you could come to for quick, satisfactory, consensual sex. *Consensual. A word you've recently learnt, Nikhil?*

He drove into the AIIMS campus and made the guard open the gates for him, thereby bypassing the entire mess at the AIIMS crossing. A quick left into the colony meant he didn't have to get onto the main road at all and could park in the relative peace of the colony instead of the madness of the market. In another life he had learnt French at the Alliançe Francaise on the main road in the vain hope that it could make him more cosmopolitan. Also, he'd thought that it would help him understand women, wine and cheese—in that order. *Fat chance.*

The market bustled and boomed in his ears. Was it just him or did it have an air of desperation to it? Customers trying to squeeze the last few drops of blood out of the shops before they closed; shopkeepers intently looking out for serious customers, hoping for the last few rupees to trickle in; snooty jewellers with gem-encrusted displays; small vendors with hair bands and plastic clips. Years ago, a man used to sell stickers and marbles, *only* stickers and marbles in front of a huge, posh shop. Juneja had wondered, even then, how he could possibly eke out a living. Today he was nowhere to be found.

He walked on to the fancy shoe shops. D&A was Sanjana's favourite. Knowing that he could be sure of not finding her in it today, he walked in. It was a trip into olfactory India. Incense sticks, sweat, leather and female perfume lay heavy on the air-conditioned air. OK, so it wasn't the smell of Arse, so perhaps it wasn't quite the smell of *all* of India. Shoe shop Delhi, perhaps.

In order to lend credibility to his visit, he looked at the footwear on display, all the while checking out the PYTs behind him in the mirrored display racks. There was a particularly delectable one, buying stilettos with her gal-pal. She had obviously found the footwear of a lifetime for the Diwali card party season coming up ahead.

'They're perfect for ethnics and Western formals!' Sounded like a case of equality.

But then disaster struck. The shoes were too small. He watched her struggle like a Cinderella sibling, trying desperately to wedge her foot in. It reminded him, in a curious way, of a fish struggling to stay under water, searching for life and being forced to gasp for air.

Had Kasturi struggled like this? Had she known she was going to die? Or had she wished to die? And Theresa Schmidt, who had committed suicide? Was she the weaker because she hadn't fought? What must it have been like to fight a rapist who doesn't speak your language? Could he have misunderstood her cries? Thought they were an entreaty to continue rather than desist?

'Sir, shall I show you the shoes?'

Startled, Juneja discovered he had been staring at a pair of white, faux snakeskin boots.

'Sir, latest design. They look very cute!'

'No, no, I was just looking.'

'Special rate for you, sir, 10 per cent discount.'

Revolted by the overfamiliar murmur in his ear and by the insult to his pocket, Juneja stalked out.

Outside, a few shops were already pulling down their shutters and Juneja realized that if he wanted to get anything done, he was going to have to get a move on.

To assuage his own conscience, he stopped at the corner and bought a packet of cigarettes. A trip to the market should not be totally in vain.

He moved on, looking cursorily at luggage shops, men's apparel and still more shoes and, realizing that this half of the market was at an end, he moved on to the crossing to get to the other side of it.

In the far horizon he could see the scaffolding going up for Dussehra. Ravana, the demon king; Meghnad, his son and wannabe demon king; and Kumbhkaran, Ravana's brother who had in fact warned Ravana but then stuck by him unlike some other people.

Juneja had always thought that instead of Meghnad, it should be Vibhishan up there. The creepy brother who'd also warned Ravana but then sneaked off to Rama. *Pious prig.* That would have been the perfect Trinity. The Good, the Bad and the Maybe. Problem was, they all get lynched. Well, they only get lynched in the Juneja version. In the real, mythological version, Vibhishan doesn't get strung up. What happens to him? Does he live forever and ever? Or does he go up in smoke? In the due course of time, or immediately? That might just be worth finding out.

12 October 1999

The buzz of his cell phone woke Juneja the next morning at nine. Wild elation at the fact that the first thing to happen this day was a telephone call was tempered by the sobering thought that it could be Sanjana. He let the phone ring and checked the caller ID after it had stopped its shrill summons. It was Khurana.

He returned the call immediately, husky, sleepy voice and all, swallowing desperately in the vain hope that he'd sound more alert.

'Hello?'

'Nikhil, thank you for calling back so fast. We have an emergency on our hands here.'

You do?

'Sarbati tried to commit suicide yesterday. She has been asking for you. Perhaps you could come and see her today. I assume you are still on leave, since you're not in office,' continued Khurana.

'Asking for me?' Juneja was appalled.

Why? Why? Why?

'Why should she ask for me?' *The next thing, she'd be saying* I'd *raped her.*

'Nikhil, she's homesick and very, very lonely. However little you know her, you have met her in her village. Perhaps she wants to talk to you about it … or about her daughter.'

What a choice!

'In any case, I suggest you get here by eleven, which should give you plenty of time to shower and breakfast. I'll try and drop in for lunch. Otherwise you can come by the morgue after you've met her.'

Bastard.

Reflecting bitterly on the injustices in life and wondering how on earth one conducts a conversation with raped women, Juneja went off to do exactly that.

He'd had a restless night and his stomach was feeling distinctly uneasy from all those kebabs he'd ruthlessly shoved in. The shower made him feel better, but the choice of clothes or 'apparel', as the twits in the shops called it, was another puzzle. Sombre, funereal white? Considering the suicide attempt, better not. She could interpret it as encouragement. Feeling-better beige? Reminded him of the uncooked kebabs, i.e., vomit inducing. Life-affirming red? Khurana would screw his happiness.

Blue jeans and a light blue shirt seemed breezy and light. Sort of fun and relaxed. Khurana of course would say something about Peter Pan and not wanting to grow up, but he'd have to grin and bear that one.

That could be a sure shot bestseller, Nikhil. A 'how to' guide for clothes. Not what to wear to a formal dinner, but when chatting up the weak and downtrodden. Interrogation garb as well as now-that-I'm-not-interrogating-you-any more-what-say-we-bonk? attire. In a friendly, non-threatening way, of course. Also, clothes that were acceptable to uncle/father types and did not solicit sardonic jibes and still made her melt and come hither instead of fleeing thither.

Khurana lived in a huge bungalow in one of the many side lanes of Connaught Place. Must be one of the few properties left in CP that was still in private hands and as such worth a gold mine.

Sarbati was sitting on the front lawn on a rug, sunning herself.

This is the life. Hang around on a prime property, drink in the sun, order a beer, chill. What's with the suicide bit?

Juneja carried over one of the rattan chairs from the terrace. No point in squatting on the grass. As he neared her, he noticed the thick bandages on her wrist.

'So, Sarbati, what is this I hear?'

Hear your own voice, Nikhil. She's a raped woman not a two-year-old, cut out the hearty, affable uncle bit.

She looked up listlessly, taking time recognizing him. He noticed for the first time that her eyes were a curious, lemony gold.

'Yes, I know, sahib. You have been kind to me. Khurana Sahib, he is also very kind. His wife also. But you know, it is not the same.'

'The same as what? As your village?' He was damned if he knew how it was pronounced. 'What is the problem? You have a roof over your head, food, drink. Do you need money?'

'Not any more.'

What the hell does that mean? 'You needed money?' *C'mon woman, let's cut the games! I don't have all day.*

She answered slowly. As if she had taken time to think the whole thing through. Each word was a philosophical observation. Juneja felt his nerves jangle each time she took a breath.

'Sahib, I thought that if I had money, I would be safe. With money I wanted to get my daughter married, secure her future. I thought if I save enough, we'll get a new roof. But now I have realized that it's not having money that makes things better. It is power. People are scared of poverty because poverty is a weakness. They think it is a disease. If they spend time with me, they will get it. Just like my caste. Touch me and you will get my caste. Touch me and you will become poor. But so long as I am poor, you can do what you want with me.

'Tell me, sahib, these men, they do things to us, to our bodies. They fuck us, they kill us with their bare hands, but only *we* are dirty? *They* are not dirty? My caste, my child's caste, that she was bleeding, this is dirty. Nobody in that village will touch us. But the men? They are clean? They don't have any disease?'

So, Nikhil, you want to put an uncle act on that? Want to give a lecture on AIDS or STDs? No? I thought not.

'No, Sarbati, it's not like that. Look at us, at me, at Khurana Sahib. We want to help you, don't we? We don't think you are dirty.'

'But Sahib, I think I am dirty. Talking to you like this about sex, about me, about my child bleeding … I would never have done it before. Now I have lost everything. My body, my child, my shame.'

'Don't talk like this. We will punish the people who did this to you.' *Yeah? How?*

'And who will you get? The Big Sahib for giving the order or the villagers for obeying it?'

Go with the flow, Nikhil, with the frigging flow. 'We will get all those who are guilty.'

Juneja pulled up in front of a kiosk before going over to Khurana. It made sense. Almost every conversation he had these days started with 'have you seen the papers?' He might as well see them before going to Khurana.

Yes, there he was, grinning amiably on the front page of the city news. What was this? Some kind of vendetta against him or what? He hadn't raped anyone. And quite frankly he was getting sick of this entire Sajjan Kumar diatribe as well.

After all, rape wasn't *all* the same. Rapists weren't all the same. Surely ol' Sajjan couldn't be compared to some rabid villager types who'd been going hammer and tongs at

Kasturi. It was absurd, this kind of silly comparison. And he wasn't going to go along with it.

He marched into the morgue feeling distinctly militant. Khurana was conducting a pre-lunch autopsy and would be strolling in shortly. Alternatively, he'd left instructions: Juneja could join him since it was after all a police case. Juneja gracefully declined and went out to the balcony for a smoke.

Khurana came out some fifteen minutes later, looking frazzled and yes, the word was rumpled. His clothes didn't have the Spartan chic one normally associated with him.

'Rough case?' asked Juneja from the door.

'Not really, just brutal. But actually it was a rough night.'

'Why?' asked Juneja, viciously stubbing out the cigarette in a potted plant before going in.

'Why? Because we discovered Sarbati bleeding at around ten o'clock at night and by the time the entire wound had been cleaned and she had been calmed down, it was after midnight. Well after midnight.'

'So what do you want me to do?'

'Nikhil, are you out of your senses? What do I want you to do? What do you want *me* to do is the question. I took in this poor woman to help you. She is severely traumatized and, not surprisingly, depressed. Have you met her?'

'I'm coming from your house. She was sitting on the lawn, sunning herself. I asked her if she needed anything, money to buy clothes, stuff. But she said no.'

Khurana sat down with a thump.

'Nikhil, she's just lost her daughter, her sister and her home. No, she doesn't want any money to buy clothes. She wants a sense of security.'

And so do I. But does anyone say, 'Yes, I'll stand by you?' Does anyone give me a sense of C Q fucking Rity?

'What does that mean? No one is attacking her in your house!'

'No, Nikhil, it's not about being attacked in my house.' He got up and went into the small attached kitchenette and returned with a thermos and two cups. It was coffee for a change. Juneja accepted it gratefully. This kind of slanging match was not what he had expected from Khurana.

Khurana drank his coffee steaming, scalding hot and poured himself another cup before leaning back with a sigh, 'You know, Nikhil, Sarbati told me that she named her daughter after Kasturba.'

'That's her mother?'

'No, that's the mother of the nation. Gandhi's wife, Kasturba Gandhi.'

'Oh, yes, I remember. So?'

'So she thought, and I realize this is naïve, but she seemed to believe that this name was a talisman of sorts. It would shield the child from harm. Instead, her daughter was murdered right in front of her eyes. Wouldn't you be traumatized by that?'

Juneja studied his shoes. 'I think it's silly to think that just because you call your child Albert, he'll be Einstein!'

'Perhaps. But the truth is, and Sarbati realizes it, that in this country, there is a different law for Kasturba Gandhi and for her Kasturi.'

'Right, so if it had been the daughter of a chief minister who'd been raped, there would be a difference?' Juneja knew the answer to that one before Khurana could answer.

'Nikhil, quite frankly, I can't imagine any circumstances under which the daughter of a chief minister could be gang raped by a bunch of villagers, but yes, if she had been, yes, I think it would make a difference. A huge difference.'

'Yes, yes, alright. But so this was Kasturi and she was fifteen and OK, I get it, she was poor and all that.'

'Yes, Nikhil, she was fifteen and I could put both my hands up her vagina.'

Sick of the repeated genital reminders, Juneja got up to go. 'And that makes a difference, Dr Khurana? That is what makes a difference?'

'I don't know, Nikhil. I'm not God, I don't know everything. But it should, shouldn't it?'

'What d'you mean "it should"?'

'Shouldn't it make a difference to you that a girl was brutalized and killed in this way? Nikhil, you're a policeman. Shouldn't you care about this?'

'It matters to me! But what d'you want me to do?'

'Nikhil, I repeat, I'm not God. You must do what your conscience demands. What you think is right.'

Khurana paused to draw breath and let loose his most lethal salvo. 'In this case as well as in the case of Theresa Schmidt. You must do as you see fit.'

You dare draw a parallel? You dare? Juneja felt his hands shake as he fought for control.

'I don't have time for this. I need to go and get things sorted out for tomorrow.'

Juneja stormed out of the hospital and strode off to his car.

And now? Where now, my pretty? Do all roads lead to Roma? Or to Arse? To professional suicide?

There didn't seem to be anywhere left to turn.

He got into the car and drove out of the parking of the morgue.

If he turned left, off the beaten path, he could befriend Sarbati and make sure, in a protracted mud-slinging fest, that justice was done. Theresa Schmidt? *Well, what the fuck. Ditto.*

He could turn right and continue to be a policeman, have a job, no girlfriend and no friends, and possibly no family. But he'd get some money from Raghu.

He could go straight home and quit the police force and join his father.

Today was Tuesday. Gupta wanted the report on Thursday. Ten o'clock, sharp. And sharp it would be.

The honk of a car behind startled him out of his reverie and with a sudden squeal of the tyres, he took off. Left, straight down the stretch and then right. Roundabouts and flyovers, slums and ministries, shacks and hotels, trees and desolation.

His head was pounding with the clamour of demanding voices. His father's gruff tones jangled with Sanjana's shrill demands. Khurana commanded justice over Sarbati's dulcet resignation. Rajiv screeched for peace and Sajjan Kumar rutted his way home. The homo freaks? Well, they at least were quiet. They just wanted to rut in peace. *Fair enough. But what about the rest?*

He discovered to his amazement that he'd really managed to drive all the way up to the Red Fort. Before he punished himself any more, he turned right into the parking and pulled over. He might as well get some Diwali shopping done. The gajak from Kinari Bazar would keep till Diwali. Plus it cost a pittance. He would treat himself to a meal at Karim's before that. The Last Meal before the public crucifixion started. Wasn't that a painting or something? Strange that Christ would stuff his face before copping it. Apparently, Jesus and he had something in common.

He got into a cycle rickshaw and let himself be pedalled into the frenzied chaos of the narrow streets and by-lanes.

Karim's was hot and delicious. Juneja managed to ruthlessly suppress any queasy feelings he might have had about his meaty dinner and chomped his way through another two plates of kebabs. If he didn't have a woman, he might as well have a paunch.

He forced himself to walk to Kinari Bazar rather than taking another rickshaw and was about to buy a vast amount of gajak when he suddenly realized that his grandmother had died and he would most definitely not be celebrating Diwali this year. He bought two kilos, telling himself that private consumption was permissible. Feeling like a royal dick, Juneja clambered into a rickshaw.

Traffic on the main road was moving at snail's pace. A huge truck had toppled over, completely blocking the narrow road. Although no one seemed to be hurt, there was no way the rickshaw would be able to get past till the truck was moved. He could of course dismount and walk, but his stomach told him, in no uncertain terms, what it thought of that suggestion.

People were milling around: some with suggestions, others to gawk. His own rickshaw driver made the suggestion that one could try and heave the truck off the road, if everyone present gave a hand. Juneja told him to shut up and restrict his energy to driving the rickshaw.

The Red Fort loomed—large and majestic—on the horizon. In a few days, it would be the background for yet another Dussehra celebration. Good would vanquish Evil. A pious Rama would tear down Demon King Ravana with his ten heads.

Juneja felt sorry for Ravana. What must it be like to have ten heads? To carry that load? Did the heads have different thoughts? Did they babble in different tongues, like the crappy voices in Juneja's head?

He handed over ten bucks to the rickshaw driver and strode off in the opposite direction. This was the notorious red-light area of Delhi. A wholesale market for sanitary ware by day and a wholesale market for unsanitary ware by night. He'd always thought it would be fascinating, till he'd done a beat there. Women who let themselves be screwed for a tenner didn't look so hot, he'd discovered.

They looked like Kasturi had done. Bottom of the heap.

His cell phone rang. The number had been withheld. *What the hell! Another voice might bicker down my valley …*

'Hello?'

'Nikhil, this is—'

'Raghu.' They spoke in perfect unison.

'Yes, Nikhil, it's me. How are you? Out of the jam?'

'Not quite,' answered Juneja truthfully, 'but I'll get there. How about you?'

'Oh, I'll get there too, Nikhil. With a little help from my friends. Are you one of them?'

Tired of the James Bond talk, Juneja answered in his usual, elegant way, 'Cut the crap, Raghu, what d'you want?'

'I was serious, Nikhil. I wanted to know if we could end this in an amicable fashion.'

'What's amicable?' asked Juneja, not entirely sure of the meaning. Amicable? Amiable? *Despicable* was a word Sanjana always used …

'More than sixty-seven lakhs.'

'What does that mean?'

'Come on, Nikhil, don't make me spell it out. We can sort this out without any more bloodshed.'

'Yours, you mean.' At least he could spill some here.

'Nikhil, please, I'm willing to be reasonable.'

'OK, so where does your reasoning take you?'

'Joshi did it.'

'He's willing to take the rap?'

'He'll go to jail in Miraat. So why shouldn't he? When he gets out, he'll get a lifetime's pension from me.'

'Muk and Moses?'

'They can come back. But if they interfere again, I won't be so nice.'

Fair enough. It at least solves their housing problems.

'Sarbati?'

'What about her?'

'Can she come back?'

'No. No, she can't.' It was the only time that Raghu's voice lost its suave assurance and betrayed emotion.

Juneja tried to maintain the upper hand. 'Scared of the pussy of your nightmares, Raghu?'

Raghu laughed. The confidence was back. 'She's the stuff *your* dreams are made of, Nikhil. You keep her. A token Arse.'

Juneja felt a wave of emotion rise. It would end this way. This was the way. The way to the left, the right one, and it led him straight ahead.

'OK, but the Joshi thing?'

'Yeah, what about it?'

'You have to make it more than a police brutality scenario. This guy,' Juneja struggled for the name, 'Ram Lal, he has to be nailed.'

'Ram Lal?' Juneja could hear Raghu struggling as well. But it was an unequal struggle.

'OK, fine, we'll nail him. A police encounter, do you mind? Jail term could be difficult.'

Walking all the while, Juneja disconnected without giving an answer. Was this the solution to all his problems? He was standing next to a shop selling Habshi Halwa. Nigger sweets. Pushing weighty matters aside, he demanded a portion to eat on the spot. It was thick, sweet and viscous. Like toffee made with copious amounts of butter.

Now what? Back to the Red Fort? Back to the problems?

Or call Raghu and earn a quick buck? Running away from them all was another option.

Hand in your resignation tomorrow. Ask your father for help. Your father, who is likely to be on your side ... maybe.

He started plodding back towards the Red Fort and came upon the rickshaw driver he'd deserted.

'Sahib, it's done!' The jubilant cry of the rickshaw driver brought Juneja back to Delhi.

'Great, let's go!' answered Juneja clambering back in.

He opened one of his boxes to celebrate. If this wasn't private consumption, what was? He crunched down on the first sweet flakes, the excessive sweetness of the past hour hurting his teeth.

So, Nikhil, have you decided? Are you calling up Raghu? It'll solve your and the M&M's problems. Sarbati? Well, it's a solution of sorts for her as well.

And what about Theresa Schmidt?

She is dead. The job is done and the bitch is dead, isn't she?

Up ahead, the Red Fort glowed red in the sun. Juneja could make out the outlines of the scaffolding before it. The effigies were being assembled for the coming festival. Good over Evil—the eternal battle. Ravana's heads lolled on the ground, waiting to be mounted. But the voices in his own head were strangely quiet. He conjured them up, one by one.

You must do what you think is right, Nikhil.

But I don't.

Which side are you on, Nikhil?

My own.

Do you know what you're doing?

No.

You don't want to help her because she's poor?

Yes.

I want to marry her.

She's dirty, she asked for it.

There you are, Nikhil, she's come into the picture as you knew she would. But she is dead, isn't she?

They all were.

Acknowledgements

I would like to thank Gotthard Hohensee for his help with the medical details and Raphael Vogt for his help in matters too detailed to list here.